Happily Ever After, Again

A Ghost Murder Mystery

D. F. Jones

Happily Ever After, Again, © 2018 D.F. Jones; Dawn F. Jones
E-book ISBN 978-1-7323054-0-3
Print ISBN 978-1-7323054-1-0
Hardcover ISBN 9798809246699

Cover Art, by Jones Media, images provided by Shutterstock © 2017
Editing by Alicia Street
Formatting by Jones Media
Published by Jones Media

Mom, I will miss you forever!

Acknowledgments

Writing Happily Ever After, Again kept me sane during the last months of my mother's life. After a long-term battle with Alzheimer's, mom passed away on April 14, 2018, in her home, surrounded by her family. Alzheimer's is a devastating disease for patients, families, and caregivers. It's a long goodbye that took place for years. My mother and I had a special bond. She was my best friend and my biggest cheerleader. Her praise boosted me until the very end of her life. I will miss my mother for the rest of my life, but her unconditional love lives on in me, my family, and my characters.

Happily Ever After, Again is the first book that I've written that she didn't read. So, it is bittersweet to share my latest labor of love. Thank you again, Alicia, my editor, for your insight, comments, and suggestions. Thank you to my beta readers and the D.F. Jones Team for supporting my work and spreading the news of my books. Your input, encouragement, and feedback keep me writing. Thank you, Amanda, for designing my cover and marketing materials. You always make my books look great.

And most importantly, to my readers, thank you for supporting and sharing my books. Your word-of-mouth referrals, written reviews, messages, and comments help me hone my craft to create new characters and stories.

Hugs!

D. F. Jones, USA Today bestselling author

Contents

Chapter 1

Eagle Creek, Tennessee

Lauren closed her eyes as the minister performed the graveside service. She couldn't register the words from the sermon or the sympathetic stares from the somber crowd of family and friends.

All she could do was stare at the dark cherry casket covered with a wildflower pall. Behind the coffin, rows of granite headstones and obelisks shimmered in the glaring sunlight, the overpowering scent of floral sprays mixed with freshly mowed grass making her nauseous.

Agonizing grief filled her soul with the permanence of death. Her physical body was numb, and an ache deep in her heart had fractured into millions of pieces. Pieces that Lauren couldn't fathom ever putting back together again.

A warm September breeze swept through her hair. She reached up and brushed the strands from her face.

The covered tent flapped against the metal poles creating a constant pinging.

It was surreal that Lauren had been ecstatically happy with the love of her life—less than a week ago. She had met Bratten at Bellamy's for their anniversary dinner. She remembered every vivid detail of the evening—etched in her memory forever.

Last week

Eagle Creek

Lauren entered the revolving door of Bellamy's and walked over to the hostess desk. "I'm Lauren Drake. My husband has a reservation for two at eight."

"Oh, Ms. Drake, he's here. Follow me." The perky brunette's short hair was slicked back behind her ears. She wore a crisp white collared shirt with black slacks. Her high heels clipped on the red brick tile floor.

The recessed lighting accentuated the dark green walls and wood trim. Crystal vases of white lilies and peonies sat on white linen-draped tables accessorized with silver and black tea lights. Long mahogany well-stocked bar lined one wall of the cozy dining room.

Around the corner, Bratten sat in a booth near the fireplace. His face lit with a smile, and he rose to greet her with a kiss. "Happy Anniversary, gorgeous."

"Happy Anniversary, darling. Have you been waiting long?"

"Nope, just long enough to order a bottle of champagne. Hard day at work?"

"Not too bad. You?"

Bratten's crystal blue eyes gleamed with excitement as he raised a brow. "I took the afternoon off, and I have a surprise for you after dinner."

Lauren's fingers tented in prayer mode. "Oh, I love your surprises. What do you have up your sleeve?"

A slow smile crept across his lips. "I might be persuaded to give you a hint if you kiss me again like no one's watching."

"Aw, you're a little devil." She pushed away from the table, sat on his lap, then cupped his face with her hands and kissed him.

The waiter coughed as he approached their table.

Lauren went to get up, but Bratten held her tightly. He looked at the waiter. "To start, we'll have the beef strip loin with truffles and wild mushrooms in the Bordelaise sauce and the au gratin potatoes. Oh, and we'll have the dessert first. The chocolate fondant with cream. It's an anniversary tradition."

"Excellent choices, sir. Shall I pour the champagne?"

"Please," Bratten replied.

Lauren's cheeks flushed with embarrassment. "Bratten, please let me go. People are staring."

"So, what. Let them. It's not every day we celebrate another year of marriage. The only thing that could top this is you telling me that we're having a baby."

"Not yet." She picked up the champagne flute and touched it to the rim of his glass. "But here's to another year of trying."

"Oh, I like the way my baby thinks." He looked at the waiter and winked.

The waiter grinned and retreated from the table.

Lauren sipped the fruity champagne, returned to her chair, and the bubbles tickled her nose. "I gave you a pretty spectacular kiss, so what's my after-dinner surprise?"

He drummed his fingertips on the tabletop. With a sly grin, he said, "Hm. First, we're going for a ride on the company jet. There's a supermoon tonight, and my new pilot is waiting for our arrival. That should take us, oh, about an hour. Then I booked the honeymoon suite at The Hamilton overlooking the Cumberland River. And I have all sorts of goodies lined up for the rest of the night." He rubbed his hands together in glee. "I took off tomorrow and called your boss, so you have the day off too. The two of us can get into all kinds of trouble."

He placed his right hand over her left one. "I can't imagine my life without you, Lauren. You took a chance on me, on us, and changed my life for the better."

Lauren kissed his knuckles, then pressed the back of his hand against her cheek. "Well, you were intimidating, and beautiful women always surrounded you. I almost didn't go out with you after my sister told me that you'd only end up breaking my heart."

With dramatic flair, she pressed her hand to her chest. "Me, a mere graphic artist, and you, the owner of a highly successful business in real estate development. We didn't exactly run in the same circles."

"You may be exaggerating a bit." He leaned back in the chair. "I'm a visible person because I'm an involved citizen. Most of the girls you're referring to jumped in the photos to get their faces in the society magazines or social media. Rarely did I have actual dates." He chuckled. "Well, except maybe with Alex." Alex Charland was Bratten's best friend, his old college roommate, and their attorney.

Bratten shifted in his seat, crossing one of his long muscular legs over the other. "I remember seeing you for the first time. I was blown away. I stopped by Smart Media to look at our new logo and collaterals. I had to meet the designer. It seems like yesterday when you sat behind your desk with an enormous Mac, biting your bottom lip, engrossed in thought. You looked up at me with beautiful brown eyes that had my insides doing backflips."

She giggled. "I froze when our eyes met. I couldn't breathe, but imagine running my fingers through your thick brown hair. We just stared at each other for an hour, and you said...."

"'Will you go to dinner with me?'"

Lauren smiled. "I said, 'I don't date clients.' And you said...."

"'It's about time for you to break that rule. No strings attached. Just dinner or drinks.'"

"I hesitated for about ten seconds, then agreed. It was something about how you looked at me that I instinctively knew we...."

"Had a connection."

She laughed again. "And you're still completing my sentences."

Lauren's senses heightened as the wait staff served mouth-watering desserts followed by the delectable main courses, and they topped off the dinner with two crème de cacaos.

She and Bratten talked incessantly about everything and nothing. Their innermost thoughts seemed to mirror each other.

After paying the bill, Bratten held her hand, walking out the door. "Leave your car in the overnight parking, and we'll pick it up tomorrow."

"I already did." She placed her hand in the crook of his arm and leaned against his shoulder.

Bratten opened the passenger door to his black AMG GLE Coupe and kissed the top of her head. "Fasten up, sweetheart," he said with his best imitation of Humphrey Bogart.

Bratten was the most romantic man she knew and funny too. "I haven't flown in the jet in a while. Who's the new pilot? And what happened to Zachary?"

"Zachary retired. Mason hired a relatively young man, Dennis Kelton. He took over Zachary's duties last month. I thought I told you." He shrugged. "Oh, well. Zachary and his wife moved to Cozumel. She has family there."

"Nice. I went to Cozumel with my family when I was in high school. I loved it."

"Have you been to Cabo San Lucas? One of my favs." He turned onto the highway leading toward his private runway.

Frowning, she said, "I don't want to hear about Cabo if you were with another female."

He threw his head back and laughed. "No, babe. I went with my software development team several years ago. Do you want to go sometime? Or we could change plans and fly out tonight."

She twisted in her seat to face him. "I have a deadline due Monday. But I have vacation saved up for a ten-day stint somewhere. Just give me the dates, and I'll request time off."

"I wish you'd quit your job, but I respect your decision to stay."

"Hmm. Someday maybe."

Bratten pulled the car into the parking spot of the hangar at Eagle Creek Airport. The new pilot had the steps down, waiting for them on the platform with a steward.

Bratten allowed Lauren to climb the stairs first. He shouted, "Thanks for having her ready, Dennis."

They boarded the jet, and in minutes, millions of flickering stars dotted the black velvet sky. The bright supermoon looked so close Lauren could almost touch it. Below, the Cumberland River rippled and glistened against the backdrop of the twinkling city lights of Eagle Creek.

Bratten brushed her hair away from her shoulder and kissed her neck, sending shivers up her spine. "Breathtaking."

Lauren turned and kissed him softly on the lips. "It is breathtaking. A night that I'll never forget."

"I was talking about you."

She lowered her eyelashes before gazing into the deep blue pools of his eyes with so much love it made her dizzy.

He leaned in and traced his fingers over the curve of her cheek. He stared so intently as if memorizing every line of her face. He lifted her chin and slanted his mouth over hers in a mind-blowing kiss that made her toes curl.

She moaned. "You are perfect, Bratten Drake."

He continued kissing her without interruption, then flashed her a brilliant smile. "Only one perfect man in human history, and they crucified him. I'll take darn good any time of the week."

Bratten brushed his soft lips against hers. His tongue licked the seams of her mouth, tasting; then, he tugged on her bottom lip. He whispered, "I knew from the first night that I wanted to spend the rest of my life with you. I want you to be the mother of my kids. You're everything to me."

He looked up and pointed. "See that patch of land on the hill with the spotlight?"

She nodded and leaned back against his chest as he wrapped his arms around her.

"That's where you and I are going to make a family. We flew to my hometown, Wycliffe. I closed the deal yesterday on one thousand acres of prime land. Wycliffe is only forty minutes from Eagle Creek and ten by helicopter if you want to keep working. I grew up in Wycliffe, and the small town is like something out of a Norman Rockwell painting. We can still keep the house in Eagle Creek if you want."

He pressed his cheek next to hers. "I envision us with three kids, two girls and one boy, two dogs, and maybe one cat. A sprawling country house with acres of land to create our slice of heaven right here on earth. Great schools too."

Lauren placed her hands over his and leaned her head back against his shoulder, tilting her gaze to meet his. "How can you be so cosmopolitan and old-fashioned simultaneously?"

He gave her a boyish grin and shrugged. "I won't deny that a part of me wishes you'd become a full-time mom, but it's your choice. I won't push my luck. It's just that my mom made my childhood special before her life got cut short. I want my kids to have a close relationship with both of us."

She took a deep breath and exhaled. "I'll make you a promise. If I become pregnant, I'll devote myself to being a good mom and wife. I'll never place my work before my family, but that's a two-way street, Bratten Drake. You must do the same. I can work anywhere that I have a computer. It may be time to think of branching out with my own design company."

"That's why I want to move to Wycliffe. I want to start over. I'm setting up a sole proprietorship in Wycliffe. There are a couple of buildings on the square that I'm looking into buying to set up shop. So, I promise always to put you and the kids first, and I love the idea of you starting a company too."

He pulled her back into his arms while she stared out the window. "Oh, and by the way, you know Rose, my assistant?"

"Yes, I know, Rose."

"Mason has been acting erratically, and last week he yelled at Rose in front of coworkers. He threw a stapler at her for crying out loud. I can't have that kind of liability in the office."

She frowned, somewhat confused. "That doesn't seem like Mason."

He softly traced her arm with his fingers before linking her hand to his. "I know, right? I talked to him, and he denied it. I told Mason that I was dissolving our LLC in Eagle Creek. He wasn't happy, but he'll be better off in the long run. I wished I'd never agreed to go into business with him but live and learn."

Changing subjects, Bratten brightened. "I want to take you to the cottage where I grew up."

"You promised to drive me to your aunt's house someday. I know you miss her, and I'd love to see it."

"How about tomorrow afternoon we drive up to the plot of land for the new house for a firsthand look-see, and then we'll stop by the cottage?"

"Sounds like fun."

His hand rested on her thigh. "A new bypass is supposed to go in on the backside of the acreage. I'm talking to the mayor of Wycliffe about developing a corridor that'll feature a golf course, condos, homes, greenway trails, and office space to complement Wycliffe's rich character with a new kind of community. I want to keep the small-town feel but with big city convenience. It'll help reduce if not eliminate the city's tax deficit and increase the incomes of everyone who lives in the town."

Taking his chin, she pulled his face closer to hers. "You're a visionary, Bratten Drake."

"Tomorrow night, we can spend the night at Wycliffe Cottage. I keep the house maintained year-round. My Aunt Lynda, God rest her soul, had the best gardens in the county. I love the old place, and you will too."

He nibbled on her ear, sending shivers up her spine as the plane circled back toward the Eagle Creek airport.

The Hamilton at Eagle Creek

After a twenty-minute drive, Bratten and Lauren checked into the hotel. Inside the elevator, he scooped Lauren into his arms, and she wrapped her arms around his neck. Lauren scanned the hotel card in a matter of moments, and they entered the honeymoon suite boasting eighteenth-century furnishings, a luxurious bedroom sanctuary with an Italian marble bathroom complete with Jacuzzi. An assortment of fruit displayed on a silver tray and champagne on ice sat on the foyer's table.

He placed Lauren's feet on the floor, and she ran over to the tall window to check out the fantastic view of the river.

"Oh, Bratten, you come up with the best surprises."

"I packed a change of clothes for us and brought toiletries from the house." He threw his keys on the side table, then popped the champagne cork. The liquid effervescence hissed and gushed into the crystal glasses. "The room has a terrace. Do you want to sit outside?"

She ran over and jumped into his arms, kissing him all over his face. He laughed again. "So, I take that as a no."

She grinned. "We have all night."

Bratten enjoyed Lauren's lack of pretense, and her inner light was a powerful magnetic force. He moved in silence, knitting his fingers with hers and bringing her over to the bed.

They sat for the longest time, just holding hands, not speaking, which spoke volumes about their level of intimacy. He'd never thought in a million years he'd find his equal. But thank God, he did.

The golden specks in her brown eyes flickered as her laughter filled the room.

He and Lauren rolled onto the massive bed, and he kissed her so deeply it was hard to breathe.

He'd lived a life without love until he met Lauren. He dated other women, beautiful women who saw only dollars signs and security. None of them had ever seen him.

Except for Lauren.

True love played a song of romance. A song of life-altering awareness that one person could affect another so profoundly. A song of such happiness made his heart soar and fluttered, skipping more than one beat.

Lauren was stunningly beautiful, but her soul kindled the spark of desire, lighting a fire of undying adoration and infinite love.

His eyes remained locked on hers as they continued playing their love song. A song given to them by the heavens struck with beautiful chords lingering in the charged air.

Lauren held his heart in her hands. Her eyes searched his eyes, so full of love and wonder. He loved Lauren on and off most of the night, and the hours stretched into the early morning.

He'd been given God's greatest gift, the gift of love, and Bratten had no intention of squandering it. He intended to cherish Lauren for the rest of his life.

The light from the full moon streamed through the tall hotel windows as Lauren stretched languorously across the bed with a smile. She reached up to kiss Bratten and panicked.

He was gasping for breath.

His lips were blue.

His skin was cold and clammy.

Lauren scrambled off the bed onto the floor, clutched her hand to her chest, and let out a blood-curdling scream. She quickly grabbed the phone and hit the concierge button.

"How may I assist—"

She cut the operator off. "My husband can't breathe. Call 911 now. If you have a doctor on staff, send him to our room at once."

She took Bratten's pulse. She didn't know if she felt one, or maybe her blood was thundering through her veins. She slipped on her robe and waited on the bed, holding onto Bratten. The door burst open with the hotel doctor, paramedics, and a couple of police officers. The doctor whisked her to the side of the room while the paramedics continued to work on Bratten for several minutes before securing him to the gurney.

The doctor said, "We're taking Mr. Drake to General Hospital. It's the closest. You may ride in the ambulance if you wish."

Hyperventilating, she gasped, "Is he breathing?"

"Mrs. Drake, please take a breath in and let it out slowly." He looked at the ground and then at her eyes. "He has a pulse."

Lauren threw on her clothes and rushed to catch up with the paramedics so she could ride with Bratten to the hospital. Her thoughts spiraled out of control.

Even though Bratten couldn't speak, maybe he could hear her. "Honey, I love you. You promised me a family. You promised me a lifetime of adventures. I'm holding you to your promises, Bratten. Do you hear me? Please, baby, open your eyes and talk to me."

They arrived at the hospital in minutes, and everything became one gigantic blur. Lauren's brain tried to process that the hospital staff rushed Bratten into the O.R. for emergency surgery.

Lauren called her family and Bratten's best friend, Alex. They stayed with her in the intensive care unit waiting room.

She wouldn't cry.

Lauren stared aimlessly across the room.

Bratten needed her.

Lauren's sister, Angeline, handed her a cup of coffee, but she heaved from the smell. "No, Angeline. I'm not thirsty. I'm not hungry. I want to know what's going on with Bratten. Please, stop hovering over me."

Angeline nodded and sat by her with her hands in her lap.

Hours passed before the surgeon stepped into the waiting room and called out Bratten's name. He led Lauren with her family and Alex to a separate private room and proceeded to tell her what transpired during Bratten's surgery.

"Mrs. Drake, your husband had a massive heart attack. But we suspect he may have been poisoned too, so I called in our toxicologist."

Lauren clutched her throat. With a shrill voice, she said, "Poisoned? How? When? I don't understand." She looked frantically at Alex and then back to the doctor. "Is Bratten okay?"

The surgeon glanced at the floor and back at Lauren, slowly shaking his head. "No, Mrs. Drake. He is not okay. Our toxicologist found traces of barbiturates, pancuronium bromide, and potassium chloride in his bloodstream."

Raking her fingers through her hair, she asked, "How is that possible?"

The surgeon continued, "Did he vomit or have any nausea?"

"Bratten was fine when we fell asleep. He was fine. Is there an antidote for the poison?"

Then the doctor changed her world.

"Mrs. Drake, your husband suffered a cardiac arrest and died. We notified the authorities. I am sorry."

She became hysterical and shouted, "What are you saying, Doctor?"

"Mr. Drake is gone."

Lauren fell to her knees and wailed. "Please, Jesus, no. Oh, please, Jesus. Please don't take him."

Alex stormed in front of the surgeon with a scowl on his face. "You have the bedside manner of a toad. I'm Mrs. Drake's attorney, Alex Charland, and Mr. Drake's. I will officially request all documentation that transpired in your hospital. Also, we request an official autopsy. I am aware of how hospitals bury their mistakes. Lauren would like to see her husband."

Alex lifted Lauren from the floor.

"No. No. Bratten can't be dead. He can't be," Lauren screamed.

Alex wrapped his arms around Lauren tightly until her sobs subsided. He carried her to the small couch in the room and sat her down.

The surgeon stiffened and said, "Of course, Mrs. Drake may see her husband. You may follow me or check-in with the nurses' station when Mrs. Drake is under control."

"Under control?" Angeline shook her finger at the surgeon. "You igmo, her husband just died."

Alex didn't know if Lauren was up to seeing Bratten, but she needed to see him, and so did he. Alex couldn't believe that his best friend for the last twenty years was dead. He neared a panic attack but focused on remaining calm with his breathing.

He lifted Lauren's chin with his forefinger. "Would you like to see Bratten?"

Lauren's face paled, and she whimpered, "I can't do this alone. Will you go with me, Alex?"

He nodded and held out his hand, which she took.

Alex gave them his and Lauren's names at the nurses' station, requesting to see Bratten.

The nurse looked up. "I'll buzz you in. Nurse Moorehead, will you take Mrs. Drake to Bratten Drake's room?"

The nurse held an iPad in her hand and nodded. "Yes, ma'am."

Alex and Lauren walked down the hospital corridor, following Nurse Moorehead.

Each ticking second was surreal.

Everything around Alex seemed more vivid, like the chatter from the nurses and technicians running to and fro checking on patients, the flickering fluorescent lighting, the beeping of the patients' monitoring equipment, and the scent of disinfectant.

Entering Bratten's room, a cold whoosh of air hit Alex, and he wondered if it was Bratten's soul or spirit. He swallowed hard as he and Lauren went to Bratten's bedside.

His best friend looked pale with a tinge of blue.

Alex had the urge to vomit and swayed with dizziness, but Lauren needed him. He gripped the bedrail, white-knuckled.

He knew the real Bratten was gone, and only his shell remained.

Alex shook from head to toe, fighting back his tears when Lauren fell apart.

"Baby, my sweet man. Oh, my darling." She bent over Bratten, kissed his lips, then laid her head on his chest and sobbed.

Alex stepped back, giving her time with Bratten. He watched the clock on the wall like watching paint dry. After a while, he went over and gently tapped her shoulder. "Lauren, we need to make arrangements for Bratten. I know some of this information may not register, but the Eagle Creek police will want to question you because of the poison found in his system. I won't leave your side. Whatever you need, I'm here for you."

Lauren fell into his arms, sobbing. "He can't be dead, Alex. Who would want to kill him?" She stilled, and her eyes widened as she placed her hand over her mouth. "Bratten and Mason argued about Rose. He told me that he was dissolving Drake Properties LLC with Mason. We were making plans to move to Wycliffe. Do you think..."

"That Mason had something to do with this?" He shrugged and replied, " I've known Mason for years. Maybe. I don't know. I knew Bratten wanted to move to Wycliffe. I handled the transactions for the new land and filed his sole proprietorship with the City of Wycliffe. You'll need to try and remember everything Bratten told you about Mason. Put it in your notes on your phone, even if you don't think it's important. Let's go, Lauren."

She looked back over her shoulder at Bratten and sobbed again, then gripped Alex around his waist, pressing her face into his chest.

Alex wrapped his arm around her shoulders and guided her out of the patient room.

In the waiting room, a detective approached Lauren, flashing his credentials.

Alex stepped forward, reached into his coat pocket, and handed the detective a business card. "I represent Mrs. Drake. She has information which may be useful regarding Bratten's death."

He said, "I'm Detective Ray Stone. Our crime investigative team is gathering evidence at the hotel. Mrs. Drake, I can't imagine, what you must be feeling, but would you mind answering a few questions at the station?"

She nodded but stared blankly at the detective in apparent shock.

Alex said, "I'll bring her in. Would you mind if she goes home, takes a shower, and changes clothes?"

"Sure thing." Detective Stone looked at Lauren. "Mrs. Drake, I knew your husband. I met him several times at charity fundraisers. He was a fine man." He turned and walked out of the room.

The last few hours had been excruciatingly hard for Alex, so he couldn't imagine the roller coaster of emotions Lauren must be experiencing.

Losing Bratten and watching Lauren spiral out took a toll on Alex.

Alex remembered the first time Bratten introduced Lauren to him. That day, he'd stared at Lauren longer than he should have, gazing into her doe-shaped eyes bewitched by her beauty, feisty spirit, and genuine soul.

But Bratten was more than just a best friend. He was the brother that Alex never had.

After a whirlwind romance, Bratten married Lauren, and he made Alex promise him that if anything ever happened to him, Alex would take care of his girl and intended to make good on his promise.

Now, Alex had the task of picking up the pieces of Lauren's broken heart.

He drove Lauren home and waited while she showered and changed.

Later in the day, Detective Stone's questioning took over an hour. Lauren sat in the station's interview room, barely talking except replying yes or no.

Detective Stone pulled Alex off to the side. "I have no probable cause to hold Mrs. Drake. But as the last person to see the victim alive, she remains under suspicion. If she remembers anything else, day or night, please call."

Alex asked, "Have you questioned Bratten's partner, Mason Williams? Bratten was in the process of dissolving his business with him."

Detective Stone placed his hand in his jacket pocket. "I'm in the process of interviewing Drake Properties employees. So,

Mr. Williams is on my list. Oh, and Alex, we'll need to schedule a time for your questioning. Mrs. Drake mentioned you as the POA of Bratten's and her affairs, is that correct?"

Alex nodded. "Yes, I am. I'll be here at eight in the morning. Will that work for you?"

Detective Stone replied, "Yeah, that's good for me too."

Alex escorted Lauren out of the precinct, then drove her home.

What a freaking mess.

Lauren's sister, Angeline, waited at the door. She wrapped her arm around Lauren and ushered her inside.

Alex said, "I have to make a few calls. I'll be inside in a few minutes."

She nodded and closed the door.

Alex withdrew his cell and hit up Private Investigator Logan Clarkson. He had met Logan at a chamber event last year and used him several times, but nothing like this. Nothing like murder. "Hey, man. We have a situation."

He filled Logan in on the details. "I need surveillance at Bratten's office and his house. I want to know Mason's every move over the last few months, and we need to put a tail on him. I want you to find out every person Bratten had contact with over the last six months."

He paused, closed his eyes, and pinched the bridge of his nose. "Clarkson? We need the same on Lauren." He hated to think Lauren had anything to do with Bratten's death, but as far as Alex was concerned in this homicide case, everyone was guilty until proven innocent.

Present-day.
Everpine Cemetery, Eagle Creek

Someone tapped Lauren's shoulder, and she blinked several times before realizing most of the people had left the cemetery.

Angeline grabbed her hand and tugged. "Come on, sweetie. Let's go to your house."

While Lauren replayed the night of their anniversary, the cemetery's maintenance crew buried her husband. She sat watching, unable to breathe, choked with emotion.

Angeline pulled her from the chair and held Lauren in her arms. "Honey, I'm so sorry. I wish I could do something to help. Know I'm here for you anytime, day or night."

Lauren just stared. She had no reply but allowed her sister to take her home.

Family, friends, coworkers, and Bratten's employees inside the house expressed their condolences. Some were compassionate: *I don't have the right words but know I am here for you if you need me.* One of Bratten's employees mentioned one of his favorite memories. But the worst response was, *I know how you feel.*

Um, no one could understand her feelings because every person grieved differently.

One person dared to mention something to the effect that since she and Bratten had only been married a couple of years, she could start over again, like not being married long lessened the pain of such a devastating loss.

One of Lauren's church members squeezed her hand. "Darling, there's a reason for everything. He's in a better place. Be strong."

At that point, Lauren wanted to scream.

She'd like to know why someone would want to take the life of such a kind soul.

After a while, Lauren offered automatic responses like an actor in a play, nodding and agreeing not to deal, almost as if she hovered in an out-of-body experience.

Bratten's partner, Mason Williams, sat down on the sofa next to her. He reached over and placed her hand in his hands. "You don't have to worry about Drake Properties. I'll make sure the business runs smoothly. Bratten was more than a partner—he was my friend. I am sorry for his death."

She'd temporarily forgotten about Bratten's business. "Thank you, Mason. I appreciate it."

As the evening wore long, most people left except her family and Alex.

Alex stared at her through the service and the wake. He had helped her so much since Bratten's death. They had a common link with the love of one person, Bratten.

As bad as she hated to admit it, something kept nagging at her. What if Alex had something to do with Bratten's death? He had control over all of Bratten's accounts.

What if it was Mason? Bratten told her he wanted to dissolve Drake Properties and move to Wycliffe.

Oh, God, her head hurt.

A terrible thought washed over her.

Whoever killed Bratten could kill her too.

Lauren couldn't trust anyone except her immediate family.

Her heart raced, and the blood pounded in her ears.

Beset with anguish.

Dizzy with a sense of betrayal and deception.

Someone she knew killed Bratten.

Her face fell forward into her hands, and she rubbed vigorously, then went into the kitchen where Angeline and her mom, Carol, washed dishes.

She started to help, and Carol said, "Darling, we'll take care of the clean-up. Do you want something to eat?"

"No, Mom. I want to sleep. I'm so bone tired that I can barely hold my head up."

Angeline dried her hands on a dishtowel. "Eron's taking the kids home, and I'm spending the night. Why don't you take a long soak in the tub, and I'll bring you a glass of wine?"

Lauren sighed. "You don't have to spend the night. I'm not suicidal." *Or was she?* "I don't want to take a bath or drink."

"I'm still staying. I can't stand thinking of you alone tonight."

"Suit yourself." She stopped and turned to her mom and sister. "I don't mean to be rude. Thanks for being with me and for helping me arrange everything. I don't think I could've managed without you and Alex."

Lauren went into the main bedroom. She had cried so much over the last several days that she was cried out. She took off her black dress, threw it over one of the two chairs, grabbed one of Bratten's shirts, sniffed his cologne, then pulled it on and crawled into bed.

Alone.

Alone.

So very alone.

Chapter 2

Before leaving Bratten's house, Mason stepped outside and made a call. "Get the brothers and meet me in the backroom of The Dirty Rat."

Noxzema said, "Sure. Want me to call the Colonel?"

"Yes, we need to talk about Drake Properties."

The Revolutionist Brotherhood bought the pub when they moved into Eagle Creek a couple of years ago. The RB was a secret organization that used legitimate businesses to carry out covert operations. After serving two tours of duty with Southern Security in the Middle East, Mason's band of brothers left and formed The Revolutionist Brotherhood.

After watching billions of taxpayer dollars get diverted to companies often owned by individuals with political agendas, the RB branched out to serve their interests. They didn't trust governments or political parties that filled the airways with propaganda bullshit.

The RB was in it not only to preserve the right to bear arms but to turn a profit. They didn't play by the rules; they made them.

Eagle Creek's position in the South, the increasing money stream made in real estate, and Rose's connection to Bratten

Drake opened the doors to a buttload of opportunities. Mason had played Bratten Drake like a fiddle at the Smithville Jamboree.

Mason walked around Bratten's house while the wake continued. He stepped into Bratten's home office and glanced around the room before going back into the living area to pay his respects to Bratten's lovely widow, Lauren. He wet his lips. Maybe the widow needed a shoulder to lean on. After speaking with Lauren for a few minutes, Mason made for the door, placing his hand on the doorknob when someone tapped his shoulder.

Alex said, "I have paperwork for you to sign. Is tomorrow good for you?"

Mason straightened his back and glared at Bratten's best friend and attorney. "I am not dissolving Drake Properties. Bratten is gone. There's no need for me to gut a cash cow. Oh, and I've lawyered up. You want a battle?" He handed Alex a business card. "Contact Jackson McCabe."

Alex let out a breath. "I don't want to fight you. I'm following Bratten's wishes. Let's give Lauren a few days to grieve, shall we?"

"Whatever, mouthpiece." Mason pushed the front door open and left without looking back. Drake Properties belonged to him. He'd be damned if some hard-on with a briefcase would take it from him.

Mason drove to his house, changed clothes, and headed for the pub. Bratten should've left things at status quo. His thoughts went to the day Bratten accepted his proposal of forming a Limited Liability Company.

Bratten looked over the prospectus, taking his time to read every word. He glanced at Mason and said, "I'm not sure about using illegals on the job sites. I've always been on the up-and-up."

Mason leaned back in his chair. "Bratten, I've told you about the living conditions of these migrants and their fam-

ilies. I know it's against the law, but you're giving families an opportunity at the American dream. You and I can help them get green cards and move their families once they're established as citizens." Mason played on Bratten's bleeding liberal heart.

"How would we take out employee taxes and provide workmen's comp?"

Mason smiled and leaned forward. "You let me take care of it. If it doesn't work out, we'll go back to your way of doing things. Come on, man, a limited liability company, is the way to go. Just sign, and I'll take care of the rest." Mason had no intention of getting green cards for the migrant workers. The whole country used illegals.

"I'll have Alex look over the agreement. We must file the necessary paperwork for the migrants, and I want to meet them. I want to make sure they have a place to live too. We can move them into Westwind's until more suitable accommodations can be found."

"Don't tell Alex about the illegals. The fewer people that know, the better."

It was Mason's first step in getting Bratten involved with the RB, but it wasn't the last.

Mason pulled into the parking lot of The Dirty Rat next to a row of Harleys. His favorite watering hole had the earmark of a classic dive bar. The rustic exterior and backyard patio gave patrons a laid-back atmosphere. He enjoyed hanging out with friends on a Saturday afternoon and drinking a few cold ones. The dimly lit interior had a long bar, dark wood paneling with sports posters and memorabilia, and a smattering of flashy neon lights from vendors no longer in business.

Midge worked behind the bar and called out, "Hi, Mason. Want a cold one?"

He nodded, and she handed him a cold PBR. No fancy-schmancy fruity beers for him. The pub offered domestics and imports. "Any of the boys here?"

She winked and pointed. "Waiting for you in the back."

Cigarette smoke filled the bar with a handful of locals playing pool while the other regulars shot the shit around tables watching ESPN on several TV screens. Flickering fluorescent lights hung over worn-out dartboards, and the smell of stale beer permeated the floors.

Mason spoke to a few of his subcontractors before making his way into the back room, closing and locking the door behind him.

His brothers sat around a sturdy Amish handcrafted solid oak table. The Colonel sat at the head of the table, joined by T-Bone, Mole, and Noxzema, each partaking of cigars and drinking pitchers of beer.

The Colonel slammed his fist on the table. "The meeting of The Revolutionist Brotherhood will come to order. Mason, you have the floor."

Mason scratched the back of his head, then pulled a Cohiba's from inside his jacket, inhaling the scent of vanilla, coffee, and cocoa. "Charland wants to meet with me on dissolving the LLC. We have a few days to think about strategy while Lauren grieves. I don't know the extent of her knowledge regarding Drake Properties, but Bratten found out about Rose cooking the books. It's enough ammo to throw us all in jail for a long time. Rose told me Bratten saved copies onto an external server. She can't find it at the office. We'll need to search his home."

T-bone leaned his forearms on the table. "Think Charland has it?"

"I think if Charland had it, we'd have an injunction to freeze the business assets. No, I think Bratten would go to great lengths to keep his squeaky-clean image." He turned to Noxzema and said, "You live down the street. Keep an eye out. Establish a pattern of the comings and goings in the Drake household. Then, search the house. Start in his office, but don't stop there. The external is no larger than a deck of cards and holds a terabyte of storage."

Noxzema looked twenty with his baby face but was closer to forty and meant as a rattlesnake with stealth investigative skills. "No problem. Lauren's never met me. I'll get in and out without detection."

The Colonel took a long pull on his beer, then set it back on the table. "I don't want any mistakes, do you hear? You're the one who brought Drake in, Mason. You know how important it is to keep our cover. The last thing we need is the feds breathing down our necks."

T-bone said, "The new shipment arrived while Y'all were at the funeral. I need you to inspect the merchandise, Mason. Can you ride with me out to the farm?"

Mason nodded. "Sure. I don't have anything else except that I filed the claim with the insurance carrier. No response yet."

The Colonel stood. "We need that bank to get the hell out of here. I gotta get back to work. I'll be in touch. Don't call me, don't text me, and don't email me until things are settled. Meeting adjourned." He left through the back door.

Mason rode with T-bone out to the farm on Mills Pond Road. Nestled in the middle of forty acres of dense woods was an old farmhouse and barn not visible from the road. The place was off the grid with no phones, no internet, or TV—a safehouse for shipments and a secure location to lay low from the law. He got out of the delivery van and followed T-bone into the barn.

T-bone opened one of the crates. "There's fully automatics, semiautomatics including some centerfield rifles and semiau-tomatic pistols. The Evening Cartel sent you a shotgun with a revolving cylinder to try out."

"Yeah, man. That's cool." Mason took out the shotgun and ran his hand along the barrel. "I'll take this one home with me. What about the other merchandise?"

"Locked in the storm cellar." T-bone went to the cellar, pushed the straw away, and unlocked the door. They went down the ladder, and half a dozen illegals sat around the small room with a living area, a twin bed, couch, and a tiny bathroom.

Their eyes widened, and Mason sensed fear.

Mason said, "*¿Habla inglés?*" One of them must speak English.

A young man in his twenties stood. "*Sí*. My name is Juan. Señor Esteban sent us to help you."

Mason smiled and shook the man's hand. "Welcome to the land of milk and honey, Juan. My name is Mr. Williams. We have housing for you and your friends. You have the weekend to settle in. There's no need to fear me unless you don't follow the rules. My lead man will place you in the crews that need help. The main thing to remember is if someone other than your lead man approaches you on a job, you repeat, no English. If they speak Spanish, go to your lead man. We, cool?"

"*Sí*, Señor. My friends want to know if we'll have access to medical care and the cash we earn. We were promised medical care in case of injuries."

Mason placed his hand on Juan's shoulder. "You bet. We have a doctor on call twenty-four seven for injuries requiring treatment. Every crew has a safety kit with first aid. *Comprender?*"

"*Sí.*"

"Juan, you work hard for us, and I promise you'll have room to move up in our organization. I'm always looking for a good interpreter on the job. Get your friends into the van outside, and we'll take you to your new home."

After securing the new crew in the back of the van, Mason looked at T-bone. "Juan will either help us or hurt us. Have the lead man report to me each day until we know Juan is on board with the plan. If he causes trouble, let me know, we'll get him deported."

"You got it." T-bone slid behind the wheel and drove away from the farm.

Weary from the long day, Mason needed sleep. His thoughts returned to Lauren. He didn't want to hurt the woman, but he would protect his brothers and preserve his way of life, no matter what.

Lauren didn't want to get out of bed. Brain fog set in over the next couple of days.

She didn't want to eat. Her medical provider had called in a couple of prescriptions for anxiety and sleep. She took advantage of both. She didn't want to deal with reality. She was still in a state of profound shock.

Every time the door opened, she expected to see Bratten's beautiful smile or hear his deep belly laugh. Every time the phone rang, she expected to hear his deep baritone voice on the other line.

Denial didn't work, either.

She was equally pissed at the world, God, or whoever snatched her husband so quickly out of her life.

The local news stations picked up on Bratten's death. Some teenage-looking reporter stated, "The police have four possible suspects in the murder case of Bratten Drake: Mason Williams, the business partner, Alex Charland, the best friend. Rose Rossi, the personal assistant, and Lauren Drake, Bratten's widow." Their faces and names were plastered on the screen at six and ten, so she turned off the TV.

How could anyone think of her as a suspect?

How could the television reporter spread vile lies with no arrests?

Lauren didn't want to face the long after-funeral checklist, but Angeline had other plans.

Lauren had given Angeline a house key. She'd come over every day and made Lauren plates of food from the gazillion casseroles jammed into the refrigerator and freezer. She cleaned the house, washed dishes, and did laundry.

On the third day, Angeline stormed into her bedroom, yanking the duvet from Lauren. "Get out of bed, right now. Get into the shower and brush your teeth, for God's sake. We have a meeting with Alex at noon."

Lauren pulled the comforter over her head and rolled away from her sister. "I don't want to. Call Alex and reschedule it."

Angeline sat on the bed, placing her hand on Lauren's hip. "You can't reschedule, honey. I wish you had more time, but you need to figure out what to do about Bratten's business. His employees are nervous about their jobs, and Mason's called several times. Alex needs to talk with you about dissolving the LLC. You owe it to Bratten to get out of bed and take care of his business."

Angeline knew how to push her buttons. She'd take care of Bratten's business.

Gritting her teeth, Lauren wanted to find out who killed him. She wanted blood.

"It's only been a few days." Lauren rolled over to face her sister.

"Lauren, it's been ten days."

"What?"

"You've been in bed for ten days. I'm sorry, kiddo, but you stink too."

A small smile crept across Lauren's face; she did stink.

She rolled out of bed and took a deep breath, then exhaled. "I'll get in the shower. Will you go with me to the meeting with

Alex? I don't want to miss something important. My emotions are all over the place."

Angeline hugged her sister tightly, then took a step back and waved her hand at her outfit. "Why do you think I'm wearing Jones of New York? I'll make you a cup of coffee. Are you hungry? You look as though you've lost at least fifteen pounds, and you were too skinny, to begin with."

"I'm not hungry. But I promise to drink a few protein shakes today."

Angeline stepped out of the room and closed the door.

Ten days.

Lauren couldn't believe ten days slipped by so fast.

She shuffled into the light gray bathroom with a brushed nickel showerhead and punched the water temp into the digital shower valve. She clicked on the LED lighting and reached into the vanity drawer to grab her toothbrush. She looked in the mirror and blinked.

Bratten stood behind her.

She turned quickly, but no one stood in the room. "I'm losing my mind."

Lauren grabbed a couple of plush white towels and hung them on the shower door mount. She stepped into the streaming water, shampooed her hair, lathered her skin, rinsed off, jumped out, and dried off with a towel.

The silent vent fans kept the steam away from the mirror. Lauren looked again, but Bratten's apparition was nowhere in sight.

She dressed quickly in a russet long sleeve tunic over a pair of black leggings and slipped on black sandals. No makeup. She pulled her hair into a high ponytail.

She padded down the long contemporary hallway with white walls. Track lighting illuminated the mounted black and white photographs of her and Bratten. They'd been so in love and happy.

Lauren aimlessly opened one of the white oak cabinets, then leaned against the white countertop next to the stainless-steel fridge.

Angeline handed her a cup of coffee. "Two sugars, two creams. I love you, sweetie, but we must go. You know how bad traffic gets downtown. I'll drive. I parked in the garage. The media hounds parked across the street. Oh, you have some sympathy cards."

"I'll let you drive." Lauren didn't want to talk with the paparazzi, nor did she feel up to driving. She sifted through the cards, and one took her breath. It looked like one of those ransom cards you'd see in a movie. Her hands trembled as she opened the envelope and pulled out the card.

I'm watching you, Mrs. Drake.

Angeline frowned and said, "What is it? What's the matter?"

Lauren was speechless. She handed the note to Angeline.

"Oh my god." Angeline opened the cabinet with the Lazy Susan and pulled out a gallon ziplock, and dropped the note into the bag. "Call Detective Stone. Now."

Lauren reached into her purse and pulled out her mobile. She called Detective Stone, and he answered. She relayed to him about the note.

He replied, "Can you come to the station, or do you need me to come to you?"

"I have a meeting with Alex. Is it okay to stop by afterward?"

"Sure. Don't tell anyone about the letter. I'll send a car to watch your place today."

"Thank you, Detective Stone." She hung up.

Angeline said, "You need to move in with us. I don't like you living here alone."

"This is my home. I still feel him here. I can't leave. I don't want to. I don't care if someone kills me. At least, I'd be with him."

Angeline grabbed her by her shoulders and shook hard. "I don't want ever to hear you talk like that again." Then she hugged her. "I'm sorry I shook you. Your frame of mind scares me."

Lauren didn't hug back. She pushed Angeline away. "I know you're scared. I'm terrified, but never seeing Bratten again is more than I can bear. Let's go talk to Alex."

Alex and Bratten had been college roommates almost twenty years ago. He passed the bar around the same time that Bratten opened Drake Properties. As the city grew, so did both of their businesses. He and Alex had remained best friends over the years, more like brothers than just friends.

Nestled in one of the few high-rises in downtown Eagle Creek, Alex's office was surrounded by trees and greenery.

Charland and Associates were displayed in black block letters on the deep charcoal entry wall. Entering the reception area, Lauren glanced around the open workspaces with glass walls and dark carpet with sleek cherry furniture, high ceilings, and recess lighting.

A young, smartly dressed female approached her. "Mrs. Drake?"

Lauren nodded.

"Mr. Charland is running a few minutes late, but he asked me to have you wait in the conference area. Please follow me."

Lauren and Angeline followed the young woman to a private conference room with an eighty-inch flat screen above a credenza next to a wall of books. She'd brought her iPad to take notes during the meeting, and the conference table's sleek design offered ample room for laptops, files, and paperwork.

The young woman said, "Mr. Charland should arrive soon. Would either of you care for water, coffee, or tea?"

Angeline replied, "Coffee for me. Cream and sugar."

Lauren shook her head no. Her nerves were frayed since she'd read the note and talked to Detective Stone. The last thing she needed was more caffeine.

Angeline waited until the woman left and whispered, "Wow. I didn't realize Alex had such a successful business. Wonder why he never married?"

Lauren raised a brow and pursed her lips. "Bratten told me that Alex just never wanted to settle down."

"Alex sure is one tall drink of water."

Alex walked into the room in a tailored Brioni suit. His dark black hair held hints of gray, setting off his brilliant green eyes. Alex's lips pressed into a tight line as he blinked away for a second.

He sat next to Lauren, placing his hand over hers. "How are you holding up?"

"Terrible. How about you?"

"The same. His death doesn't seem real to me yet, so I can't imagine how you feel. But I will tell you, Bratten had his affairs in order. He was one shrewd businessman and has made provisions for you for the rest of your life." He looked over to Angeline and said, "Thanks for coming with Lauren today."

Lauren handed Alex the note.

He grabbed a tissue, carefully removed the note, read it, and put it back in the bag.

"Did you call Detective Stone?"

"Yes, we're heading over to the police station after leaving here. Do you have any ideas?"

Alex took a deep breath and exhaled. "The only person with a motive that I know of is Mason. You have a controlling interest in Drake Properties. You decide to dissolve or stay on. I recommend dissolving the business."

Lauren became furious. "I won't allow someone to bully me. If Mason had anything to do with Bratten's death, the best course of action is to work at Drake Properties. I want to go through Bratten's files."

Alex said through gritted teeth, "It's my responsibility to watch out for you."

She stood. "You're not my father. You're my attorney."

Alex came to his feet, staring into her eyes so intensely it caught her breath. "Your husband made me promise to watch out for you on more than one occasion. I don't know if he was in danger at the time of his request, but I intend on making it my business to take care of you and keep you safe."

Their eyes locked, their breathing labored—each searching for something she couldn't put her finger on.

Angeline stood between them. With her stern mom's voice, she said, "Sit down. Settle down. You two at each other's throat isn't helping this emotional situation. Let's redirect this meeting to the reason we came today."

Alex broke eye contact with Lauren and handed them booklets. "Look, until the police finalize their investigations, we'll concentrate on settling Bratten's personal affairs. He has no living relatives, so Lauren, you're named as the sole heir. I know none of this ordeal is easy. It's like living in a nightmare."

Alex opened his folder. "As Bratten's POA, I have the original legal documents inside your portfolio. I've placed copies of his death certificate, social security card, birth certificate, marriage certificate, insurance policies, and titles, including financial info. I filed the necessary paperwork to place his assets into your name."

He shifted toward Lauren. "Regarding Bratten's business, you do have the option of overseeing the day-to-day operations. I called Mason, and he's balking on dissolving the LLC. Bratten wanted to move his business to Wycliffe, but you have a controlling interest. You're right. It's your decision. Your company, but my gut instinct tells me that Bratten's decision to start over set into motion the events that took his life. I can't prove it. It's my theory."

Lauren thumbed through the pages of the legal mumbo-jumbo, then looked at Alex. "We were making plans to build a home in Wycliffe. Bratten had plans for a new development. I want to see that through. But first, I want to

investigate   his   office.   I'll   be
c   a   r   e   -
ful."

Alex seemed agitated as he ran his fingers through his hair. "I can't stop you."

Lauren swallowed hard as tears welled in her eyes. "Bratten trusted you, and that's enough for me. I resigned from my position with Smart Media this morning. I will run Drake Properties and see his dreams realized in Wycliffe. I'll trust you to help me navigate the stormy waters with Mason."

Alex closed the folder. "Lauren, you know I'll help you any way I can. I don't say that offhandedly either. I mean it. Bratten loved you more than anyone on this earth. I spent a lot of time with Bratten at his home, Wycliffe Cottage. It's where he grew up with his Aunt Lynda after his mom died. It might be a nice place to get away for a few days. It's yours now."

The whole legal business of settling Bratten's affairs made Lauren nauseous. She didn't want to think of their property as just hers. It hurt too much. "We planned to drive up the next morning and spend the weekend at Wycliffe Cottage, but he died. No, I take that back. Someone murdered him."

Lauren felt as though someone poured gasoline into the open wounds in her heart and set fire to her emotions. "Why would anyone want to kill him? Greed?"

He squeezed her hand. "I don't know, but I hired a private investigator, Logan Clarkson, to consider every aspect of Bratten's life before the evening of his death. I've given him a liberal allowance. He's working with The Hamilton to search footage of that day and night. Something will turn up."

Angeline tilted her head. With shyness, she said, "To be honest, I wondered if you had anything to do with Bratten's death. I mean no disrespect, Alex, but you handle everything for them."

He smiled at Angeline. "Well, if we're honest, I suspect everyone who knew Bratten."

Lauren's eyes widened, and her hand flew to her chest. "Including me?"

He shrugged. "It's only natural to think of those closest to Bratten as suspects."

Angeline placed her forearms on the table, extending her fingertips toward Alex. "It doesn't seem real. It's like we're watching some *Dateline* episode, and it keeps repeatedly playing in my mind. Look, someone did it. Someone wanted Bratten dead, and Lauren could be next. I'm worried about my sister."

Lauren slumped back in the chair, consumed with grief. Someone was watching her. Her head lolled back against the chair, and she closed her eyes, her mind spinning as her world turned upside down and inside out.

Alex stood. "I'm calling Logan Clarkson. I want to tell him about the card. With your permission, I'd like to hire a security guard for you, Lauren."

Lauren shook her head. "No. No. Detective Stone is sending a car to watch my house. I don't want a bodyguard."

"Sister, that's not being smart." Angeline narrowed her eyes.

"Look, guys, I'm already freaked out enough. And what if you hire someone who happens to know the killer or maybe even works for them?"

Angeline said, "You're paranoid."

"I've got a right to be paranoid."

"Let Logan delve into the case, and we'll see what happens," Alex said. "Drive to the cottage. I have the keys. Give me a minute." He left the room.

Angeline placed her hand on Lauren's forearm. "Wycliffe is close to Mom and Dad's house in High Point. Let's drive up this afternoon after you meet with the detective. Eron's picking the kids up from school. He knows I'm with you today."

"Eron's a good man."

"No arguments from me. Eron loves me. Bless his heart. It's a nice warm day. It'll do you good to get away even for a few hours."

"Yeah, maybe. Oh, Angeline, I miss Bratten so bad it hurts to move."

"One minute, one hour, one day at a time. There're no rules on grieving. You have Eron and me, Mom and Dad, and Alex. I like him."

Alex stepped through the double glass doors. He knelt beside Lauren and took her hand in his. "Bratten loved you very much. You know that, right? He'd want your happiness and your safety. You give me the word, and I can arrange a bodyguard."

"Not yet. It gives me the creeps. I know Bratten loved me. Bratten was larger than life. My life with him was large. I cannot believe I'll never see him again. I can't believe it." Alex pulled her into his arms and held her tight. "Every time I think I'm cried out, I start all over again."

Lauren looked up into Alex's eyes, and he handed her his handkerchief. "You're a true friend."

"Here's the keys to Wycliffe Cottage. Oh, is it okay if I stop by and check on you from time to time? I'll call first."

Lauren took a step back. "Alex, you don't have to call first. You stop over anytime. Besides, I may not answer my phone."

"Thank you for your help." Angeline shook Alex's hand. "I'm glad Lauren has a strong shoulder to cry on."

Lauren grabbed Bratten's portfolio. "Well, thanks again for your help."

She and Angeline left the law office.

Lauren started to say something inside the elevator when Angeline pressed her forefinger to Lauren's lip. "It was a Freudian slip. A strong shoulder to cry on, ugh. I sometimes run off at the mouth, and you know it. I'm sorry."

"Did you see the look on Alex's face?" Lauren chuckled.

Angeline waggled the key. "Wycliffe Cottage awaits. Er, well, after you meet with Detective Stone."

Detective Ray Stone

Ray drove up to East Main Street and hooked a right onto Lytle Street. He waited for the traffic light to turn green, then proceeded to the City Center parking garage. He parked on the bottom floor and walked up two flights of stairs to street level every day. The police department location was sandwiched between the City Center and the new library.

Walking through the double doors, he stopped by the new communication room. Behind the sliding glass door, Dorothy looked up and smiled. He hoped she'd go to dinner with him one day. "Hey, Dot, how are things going this afternoon?"

She leaned in. "Big wreck out on 231. Those frigging rock trucks ran over another vehicle. Life flight took two of them to the ER while an ambulance and fire truck remained on the scene."

He sighed. "Man, I hate that. Any fatalities?"

"None reported."

"That's a good thing. Hey, I'll stop by before you head home today."

She leaned back in her chair and said, "Ray, why don't you go ahead and ask me out. What's the worst that could happen?"

Ray glanced over his shoulder to make sure no one was listening, then turned to Dorothy. "Worst case scenario, you say yes, then I screw it up somehow."

"We won't ever know, will we, if you don't ask." She slid the window shut and tapped away on her keyboard.

Ray had married and divorced before the age of thirty. Just thinking about a relationship or even going on a date made him skittish. He'd placed Dorothy on a pedestal in his mind. He didn't want to destroy the perfect illusion. Glancing at his watch, he quickened his step.

Bratten Drake's widow should arrive any minute.

Ray veered off the left hallway and went inside the squad rooms. Six detectives worked homicide. The chatter among several detectives stopped as he approached his desk.

Ray scratched his eyebrow before placing his palm on the desk. "I need the conference room for a few minutes. Lauren Drake's coming in."

Oohs and ahhs from Pete, Alvin, and Ben.

With a smirk, Ray said, "Knock it off. She's a widow."

Pete pushed away from his desk and placed his hands behind his head. "So, need any help with the widow?"

Ray looked up as an officer ushered Lauren inside the conference room. "No, but I would like you to look at my case files. Bratten's death just got more interesting this morning. Someone tampered with the hotel footage."

He leaned on the edge of the desk. "Around two a.m., Bratten left the hotel room and went into the vending area, and he never left, based on the footage. Someone edited out around an hour. The next people videoed in the corridor were the paramedics and the officers around three. Someone gained access to the hotel footage or worked for the hotel. So, how did Bratten end up back in his room without Lauren waking up? Did he make it back there on his own? Or did someone help him? And, how does the widow fit in? Suspects keep piling up. I made you a copy. Catch." Ray threw Pete the thumb drive.

Pete placed the flash drive into his laptop. "I broke down the evidence, facts, and suspect files and compiled the info into the booklet for easy reference. Forensics didn't find a single shred of DNA. No hair or fibers except Mrs. Drake's. No witnesses. A cunning killer committed this crime."

"It wouldn't be the first time a wife offed a spouse." He scratched his chin in thought.

Pete clicked away on his keyboard. "Initially, the coroner thought the victim was poisoned from chocolate strawberries, but during the autopsy, she found a puncture wound on the side of the neck. I'll review your files. Beers later?"

Ray shrugged. "Maybe." He grabbed his other notebook and stepped into the interview room, shutting the door behind him.

Lauren Drake seemed nervous, biting her bottom lip and tapping her heels on the floor.

"Mrs. Drake, thanks for coming in today. Did you bring the letter?"

Lauren withdrew the card from her purse.

He went to the desk drawer and withdrew latex gloves. "Who touched the card?"

She frowned. "Well, I suppose my mail carrier, Angeline, Alex, and me."

"Good to know. I'll get it to CSI."

He pulled out a chair next to her, placing his notebook and tablet on the table. The widow was a beauty. He had to admit.

"Did you know that your husband's partner, Mason Williams, was arrested in a Ponzi scheme in Las Vegas before moving here? He was acquitted."

Lauren's eyes went wide, and she gasped. "No. Do you think he killed Bratten? Do you think the murder has something to do with the property development in Wycliffe? Or the fact that Bratten met with him about dissolving the LLC?"

Ray jotted down a few notes. "Hm. You said in an earlier statement that there was some altercation Mason had with Bratten's assistant, Rose Rossi, correct?"

Lauren straightened in her chair. "Yes. Bratten said that Mason yelled at Rose and threw things in the office. Mason denied it. Why?"

Ray leaned back in his chair. "How long has Rose worked for Bratten?"

"I'm not sure." Lauren frowned. "I think around two or three years."

Ray bit the inside of his mouth. He didn't know how much to reveal, but he needed Lauren's trust. "Mason denied the allegation regarding Rose. He stated Bratten dated Rose a few times before he hired her and that Rose had a kid to support, so Bratten gave her a job."

He watched Lauren's face pale. The pulse in her throat throbbed.

"Bratten dated Rose before we were married?"

So, Lauren didn't know about Rose. Interesting. Very interesting.

"I haven't corroborated Mason's statement. Did you know Rose set up the evening for your and Bratten's anniversary? Bellamy's and the suite at The Hamilton?"

Lauren's face went into the palms of her hands. He looked around for tissues when she stood up and knocked the chair over with a loud clang against the linoleum floor.

She narrowed her eyes at him. "Are you implying my husband was having an affair with Rose? And she has something to do with his death?"

The guys in the office turned to face the conference room. Ray went over and closed the blinds.

He scratched his freshly shaved chin and turned to face her. "No, ma'am. I'm trying to establish a motive. This is what I do know. You've inherited a vast fortune from your husband, and Alex Charland controls that fortune. Bratten's soon-to-be ex-partner is in the position to take over his business, and Bratten's assistant was personal to him."

"Do I need an attorney, Detective Stone?" Lauren tapped her foot on the floor in apparent agitation.

"Mrs. Drake, my gut tells me you're innocent, so I will find the killer if you trust me."

Lauren hugged herself. She was shaking— part of him wanted to comfort her and tell her it would be okay, but that was against protocol. Still, he wondered how much she knew. Was it enough to get her killed?

"Detective Stone, do what you must. I want justice for Bratten's death. You'll have my complete cooperation." She allowed her arms to fall to her sides. "I want Bratten's killer."

"I sent a car to watch your place. You have my card, so feel free to call me day or night. I'll walk you out."

Ray escorted Lauren down the hall corridor toward the front of the station. Another officer ushered in a criminal in handcuffs. He caught the stench of alcohol and body odor as they passed them.

Out in the waiting room, Lauren's sister stood.

"Thank you, Detective," Lauren said.

"You can thank me when we have someone behind bars. Good day to you, Mrs. Drake."

Ray nodded to her sister, then went back through the door to his office. He thought of Alex Charland. The last thing he wanted was some high-powered attorney finagling with the Drake murder. He made a note to keep tabs on Charland too. He'd learned from past mistakes and didn't intend to stop until the Drake case wrapped.

Lauren was furious.

Bratten and Rose?

Had they been lovers?

Angeline had to double step to keep up with Lauren's strides. "What happened in there, Lauren?"

"Wait until we get in the car." Her lips pressed into a thin line.

"Take a deep breath and exhale, then tell me what is going on."

Lauren rubbed her sweaty palms on her thighs. "The good detective has four suspects." She relayed to Angeline the gist of the meeting.

Angeline gripped the steering wheel and looked at her. "He can't think you had anything to do with Bratten's death."

"Out of the four, I'm on the bottom of the list. I'll call Alex and see if he'll ride with me tomorrow to Wycliffe. I want to schedule a meeting with the mayor and find out as much as I can about Bratten's new development. I also want to pick Alex's brain about Rose. I still want to go to the cottage today, but I want to stop at the office store to buy some moving boxes and tape? I want to pack up some of his things. Can you believe Rose? I just can't believe Bratten never told me about her."

"Sure, we can drive up anytime you want, but don't confront Rose. Leave it to the police." Angeline turned onto the highway toward the mall. "And, I wouldn't put much stock in any relationship with Rose. If Bratten had wanted her, he wouldn't have chosen you. He adored you."

Lauren swallowed hard. "I feel sick. My head hurts too."

"No wonder. You sit in the car, and I'll get the supplies; then, we'll go to Bratten's office. I don't want you in there alone. For goodness sake, there's a killer on the loose."

"Here's my credit card. Get three boxes. That should be enough for the small stuff."

Angeline pulled into a parking spot and grabbed her credit card and purse. "I'll be back in a few."

Lauren watched Angeline practically run into the store, then reached into her purse and pulled out her phone to call Alex.

Alex answered on the first ring, and she rattled off the info from the meeting with Detective Stone. "Do you think you could arrange a meeting with those in charge of approving

Wycliffe Avenue? I don't think it was a coincidence that Bratten was killed after announcing the project."

"I'll place a call to the mayor and try to set up a meeting for tomorrow morning if he has the time," Alex said. "I'm sure the spearhead committee members will want to meet you. Plan on me picking you up in the morning around eight-thirty unless you hear otherwise."

Her head leaned against the car window. "Alex, will you tell me about Rose?"

"I'll tell you what I know tomorrow. Hey, kiddo, Bratten loved you and only you. Don't forget. See you in the morning."

"Okay, thanks, Alex."

A half-hour later, Lauren and Angeline arrived at Bratten's office just before the close of business. Several of the employees were leaving for the day as Angeline parked.

"Should I say something to Rose?" Lauren asked.

"N.O. I understand, though. I'd want Rose out of there too."

Lauren and Angeline grabbed the boxes out of the trunk and walked along the sidewalk. The front door was locked, so Lauren entered the PIN on the keypad to open it.

Inside the front office, framed prints of Bratten's developments hung on the walls, and a crystal curio cabinet displayed Bratten's awards over the years. A large framed photo of Bratten hung in the center of the wall, along with several pieces of Lauren's artwork. Her heart lurched at Bratten's beautiful face.

No one sat at the receptionist's desk.

She glanced back at Angeline. "I'm not sure who's still here. Let's go to Bratten's office." The door was ajar, so she pushed it open. Rose sat behind Bratten's desk, clicking away on his computer.

Rose glanced up with a look of surprise. "Lauren? What are you doing here?"

She placed the boxes on the tan leather sofa next to the back wall. "The question is, what are *you* doing in Bratten's office using *his* personal computer?"

Rose blinked several times and stammered, "I was checking Bratten's agenda. He has appointments on the books."

"I'm taking over Bratten's office and his appointments. And, wouldn't you have his calendar on your computer?"

Rose's eyes widened. "What do you mean?"

"Just what I said. Wouldn't you already have Bratten's agenda?" Lauren walked over and placed her right palm down on Bratten's desk. "This is my desk now. That's my computer, and I'm your new boss. I want a list of the people that you've contacted."

"Yes, Mrs. Drake. Ah, is there anything else?"

Lauren wanted to claw Rose's eyes out but kept her composure. She had to bide her time investigating the office, searching for clues regarding Bratten's death. "No, thank you, Rose. I'm sorry if I seem rude, but I met with Alex and Detective Stone today. I'm a little on edge."

"Oh, yes. Me too. I mean, I have an appointment with the detective in the morning. I may be a few minutes late. Yesterday, the ECP had a warrant to search Drake Properties. Mason permitted them. I still can't believe that Bratten is gone." She quickly swiped tears away from her eyes. "I'm sorry, Lauren. I'll do whatever I can to help you."

Lauren asked, "Is Mason here?"

"No, ma'am. He left about thirty minutes ago."

"Okay, I'll speak to him later. Before you leave this evening, would you mind getting me any information on the Wycliffe Development? I'm driving up tomorrow with Alex."

"The land plat is pinned to the wall." Rose pointed to the right side of the room. "Bratten's correspondence with Mayor Lane, Riley Gates, Brady Weber, and Rick Kirkland is on his computer. Just key in Wycliffe Avenue. You'll find everything you need."

"Do you have the logins for Bratten's accounts?"

"Yes, ma'am. I'll make you a copy before I leave."

"Thanks again." Lauren intended to change every password.

"You're welcome." Rose left the office and shut the door.

She ran the palm of her hand over the smooth surface of the cherry desk gleaming with furniture polish. A framed photo of her sat on the left, Bratten's sleek monitor in the middle, and the phone system on the right.

Angeline sat on the couch watching her. "Well done, baby sister. But watch out for that one. My bullshit meter went off the scale with Rose's routine. And if I were you, I wouldn't allow her to bring you coffee. I'll make some inquiries at church to see if we can find you a new assistant."

"I thought the same thing. It looks like trips to Starbucks are in my future." Lauren walked to the wall with the plat of land Bratten wanted to develop in his hometown. She traced her fingers along the lines and stopped. Her breath caught. Bratten had drawn a heart on the land where they were supposed to build a home and a life.

All gone.

She placed her hand on her forehead. "Angeline?"

"Yes, darling."

"Are you too tired to drive to Wycliffe Cottage?"

"Not at all."

"Help me pack up some of Bratten's items. The rest I can go through later. I'm going to the restroom, and then we'll take a road trip."

Lauren went to the facilities next to the breakroom. Before she entered, the hair on her neck rose. She turned left and right. No one. But she still felt like someone was watching her.

She stepped closer to Mason's office and heard whispers. Rose said that he'd left thirty minutes ago. Lauren knocked on the door, and no one answered. She tried the doorknob, and it was locked.

Lauren agreed with Angeline. Rose's bullshit meter was off the charts.

Chapter 3

Where am I?

Bratten milled among others in a vast space cast in a soft fuzzy white light. Someone approached him, and he blinked a couple of times before calling out, "Mom?"

Nancy, his mom, didn't walk as much as she glided over the surface to where he stood. She hugged and kissed him. "Bratten, my baby boy."

"Mom, am I dreaming?"

She placed the palm of her hand on the curve of his cheek. "No. You've crossed into the afterlife."

"Nooo. I can't be dead. Oh my god, Lauren. Where is she?"

"Relax, son. Crossing over takes some acclimation, but you'll have answers to every question you've ever wanted to ask once you do. Secrets of the Universe are available to you now. You may travel to realms unknown to Earth."

"No, you don't understand."

"No, child, you don't."

She held his hand, and they materialized inside the Wycliffe Cottage. The country house reminded him of a fairytale cottage with two levels, exposed beams, hand-cut wood plank flooring, and a window that spanned the entire wall, opening a beautiful view of the wooded backyard.

Aunt Lynda stepped out of the kitchen with a tall glass of iced tea. She grinned, standing under the custom doorframe with a stained-glass transom. "Here, Bratten, drink this. I remember being thirsty when I crossed over. What about you, Nancy?"

Bratten threw up his hand. "Excuse me. Just so that I'm clear. I'm dead. I died?"

Nancy tilted her head at an angle to look up at him. "Honey, no one ever dies. We move on to new life, a new journey."

"I don't want to move on without my wife. I had a wonderful life. I found the woman of my dreams. Aw, Mom, Aunt Lynda, she's a peach." Bratten thought he should be in full panic mode in the back of his mind, but oddly enough, he wasn't upset that he was dead.

Nancy and Aunt Lynda held hands and looked at each other lovingly.

Aunt Lynda said, "We saw her in your dreams."

"What? You can see my dreams?"

Nancy said, "Correction. Could see your dreams, and not all of them, son. Some dreams no mother should ever watch."

"Ain't that the god's honest truth." Aunt Lynda laughed as she sat down in an oversized, overstuffed rose-covered chintz chair.

"What happened to me?"

Nancy sat crossed-legged on the oriental wool rug and patted her hand. "Join me on the floor."

He sat next to her and noticed Nancy was a young woman again. Not the mother in his memories, but the woman in her wedding photo.

"Please tell me what happened, and I need to know what's become of Lauren."

Nancy scratched the side of her face and wrinkled her nose. "Um. I'm not sure how much you're ready to hear, but you were murdered. Lauren buried you in Everpine Cemetery next to me. Ah, and, um, we're here because Lauren and her sister are pulling into the drive at Wycliffe Cottage."

He ran his fingers through his hair in frustration. "Murdered? How? Is Lauren in danger?"

Nancy placed her hand on his forearm. "Massive heart attack by chemical injection. Lauren and her sister just pulled into the driveway."

"How do you know Lauren's here?"

"Existence is a two-way mirror. We're on this side, and the living is on the other. We brought you here for closure so that you can move on. We may move between realms as long as we don't interfere with the living." She shook her finger at Bratten. "I know what you're thinking. You can't interfere with her life."

Bratten kept calm and smiled at his mother and aunt. Neither of them had ever denied him anything when they were alive. "Mom. I made bad decisions. My decisions could hurt Lauren. I must do something. Surely, I can protect her somehow? How does one move between realms?"

"Turn around. Lauren's walking into the front door," Nancy replied and pointed to the foyer.

Aunt Lynda leaned over and whispered, "There are ways, Bratten, but it could cost your soul."

He glanced at his Aunt. "It's my fault."

Bratten turned toward the door, and the sunshine of his life walked into the room—Lauren.

He walked over to her and stared into her anguished face. Lauren had lost weight, and dark circles were under her eyes. He touched her face, and Lauren's hand flew to her cheek.

Aunt Lynda said, "No. Bratten."

Lauren turned to Angeline. "Did you feel that?"

Angeline walked into the den and placed her purse on the sofa. "Feel what?"

"It felt like a hand pressed against my cheek."

Nancy said, "Tread softly, son. She's among the living. It could cause her irreparable psychological problems. She's distraught over losing you and not knowing who or why someone killed you. Remember, most of the living don't understand the paranormal aspects of the dead."

Bratten stared at Lauren as she looked at his photos as a kid. "She felt my hand, Mom."

"Yes, she did."

"Can she see me? Hear me?"

"You must think of her, son. Yes, you may appear to her. She may even hear you if she has an open mind to the supernatural world, but you must ask yourself, do you want this for her or yourself?"

"Mom, while she's here, allow me to be with her in peace."

In less than a heartbeat, his mom and aunt vanished.

He followed Lauren throughout the house, and she went up the stairs alone and opened the door to his old room. She sat on the bed and closed her eyes.

"Bratten, I miss you so much. You promised never to leave me. You promised. I need you."

Bratten sat on the bed next to her and whispered, "I'm here, Lauren."

"Are you?"

"I will never leave you, my love."

She stretched out on his bed, wrapped her arms around his pillow, and wept.

"Don't cry, Lauren. I'll find a way." He placed his hand on her low back.

"How? You're dead. I buried you. I'm losing my mind talking to someone who isn't here."

Angeline knocked softly on the door and peeked inside. "Honey, who are you talking to?"

"Bratten. Don't look at me like I'm pathetic. I feel him, I tell you." Lauren sat up and narrowed her eyes at Angeline.

Angeline sat in Bratten's lap, melting through his molecules to the bed. "Maybe it's because he grew up here."

"Maybe. I feel peace here."

"I can understand that. Let's check out the backyard. I noticed a creek, and the gardens from the windows look incredible. Bratten's aunt must've had a green thumb."

Aunt Lynda materialized in the room. "Ooh, I like her sister, smart woman."

Bratten released a sigh. "I have to warn Lauren. Aunt Lynda, if you know-how, show me."

Aunt Lynda circled her arm around his waist as they followed Lauren and Angeline to the backyard. "Son, if you stay with her, you're haunting her. You're a ghost to her and nothing more."

"I don't want to haunt her, but she needs a warning."

"It won't change the fact that you're dead. There're risks. If you're willing to take them, I'll show you how. Some spirits choose to stay on earth. They've learned how to manipulate the elements."

Eagle Creek

The alarm clock sang its annoying song jostling Lauren out of a troublesome sleep. She reached over and hit the stop button. Six-thirty in the morning was too early for a night owl.

Lauren went into the bathroom, pulled a washcloth from the cabinet, and shuffled into the kitchen. She opened the fridge door, pulled out a bottle of Dickinson's Original Witch Hazel, and poured some contents onto the washcloth. Sitting on the kitchen loveseat, Lauren tilted her head back and placed the cold towel on her severely swollen eyes.

Fifteen minutes later, she stepped into the shower and allowed a little extra time bathing. After drying her hair, Lauren applied makeup with care then she opted for a lilac linen summer suit for the Wycliffe meeting.

The doorbell chimed. Lauren glanced at the clock. Alex was right on time. She quickly brushed on light pink lip gloss and slipped on a pair of summer sandals. She frowned, making a mental note to book a pedicure.

Opening the door, Alex smiled. Something about his intensity reminded her of Bratten. She missed Bratten every second of every day, twisting her insides.

"Good morning, Lauren. Are you ready to become a gladiator in property development?" Alex stepped inside, and his fingers brushed against hers, sending an electric shock through her body.

"You shocked me."

He chuckled. "I have that effect on some people."

"I need a cup of coffee first. How about you?" She went back into the kitchen, and Alex followed.

"Nah, that stuff is bad for you." He leaned against the counter wearing a Kiton blue and navy plaid suit, crisp blue striped shirt, and blue tie and looked like he had just stepped off the cover of *GQ*.

"Well, I couldn't survive without a little daily jolt of java. I didn't sleep well last night. So, I logged into Bratten's laptop and read his prospectus on Wycliffe Avenue. I haven't taken any recent finance classes, but I guess I know enough to be dangerous. I reviewed the land plat and Bratten's ideas for developing the property. So, I suppose I'm ready to meet the gladiators, and in the process, maybe we can find clues to Bratten's death."

Alex bowed. "Your chariot awaits."

On the drive to Wycliffe, Alex listened to Lauren describe her interview with Detective Stone. He said, "I believe Detective Stone is doing his job looking for the killer. He doesn't know either of us well enough to know we're not capable of harming Bratten."

Alex briefly glanced at Lauren before returning his full attention to the road, clocking miles while passing rolling hills and open pastures, some with livestock and others with big round bales of hay.

Detective Stone had tried placing doubts about Lauren in his mind. But he knew her relationship with Bratten. Their love seemed genuine. He decided to focus on their schedule for the day, but he couldn't help noticing Lauren's beauty.

Lauren shifted in the seat and placed her forearm on the console. "Alex, tell me about Rose. Bratten never mentioned a relationship with her."

He tilted his head and grimaced. Oh, lord. He wondered if she'd find out about Rose. "Well, that was a long time ago. Let's see, um, Bratten and I had attended a fundraising event for the humane society. Bratten placed bids where Rose worked one of the silent auction tables. Her husband, Andre, was stationed in Afghanistan."

"Her husband?"

"Yeah. Bratten struck up a conversation with Rose, and by the end of the event, he'd hired her. He wanted to help her family. Andre was killed in action seven months later, and she was pregnant."

"What? Is her son Bratten's?"

"I don't think so. I'm pretty sure Rose's husband was on leave during that year's holidays. Bratten didn't tell me anything otherwise. I think he felt sorry for her."

He clenched his jaw. "One evening, Rose and Bratten were working late and talking about her husband. She broke down, sobbing. He tried to comfort her, and things got out of control.

They didn't have an affair as it was more about him comforting a lost soul."

"But you don't know for certain. Bratten could've had an affair with Rose. She still works there. Oh, god, should I have a DNA test done?"

"Whoa, you're getting way ahead of yourself. You and I both know Bratten well enough that he would take care of his son if he had one. He wanted kids."

Lauren bit her bottom lip. "Oh, I know how bad he wanted kids. I couldn't get pregnant. We tried."

Lauren leaned against the car door and stared out the front windshield. "Thank you for telling me. Do you think Rose could've killed Bratten? Jealousy is an ugly monster."

He didn't want to tell Lauren that Bratten paid Rose more than the average personal assistant. He often gave her money with no questions asked. "I don't know."

She looked at him. "I'm going to find out."

"I don't think Bratten wanted to tell you anything to cause you pain. He had a big heart. Bratten wanted you happy because you were his light in this world. He was so excited about the Wycliffe Avenue project. He wanted to create a home for you and raise his family here."

Alex took a right off the ramp toward downtown Wycliffe driving along the scenic route. The vivid blue sky and slow swaying trees made Alex reminisce about the fun times he and Bratten once shared in the quaint college town. Wycliffe reminded him of the movie *Pleasantville*. Clean and uncluttered with ample green space.

The charming historic town had a gazebo bandstand in the center of the square where music flowed like water on Friday nights, and everyone knew each other by name. Many went to the same church on Sunday and shopped at the same grocery store back in the day.

Alex parked. He wanted to take away Lauren's pain. He reached over and squeezed her hand.

Lauren's eyes locked with Alex, and something shifted in his chest. No doubt, she was beautiful, but that wasn't the attraction. He'd fallen for her long ago, but she fell in love with Bratten, so he buried his feelings so deep in the attic of his mind. But those feelings kept rushing to the surface, making him feel like he was betraying his best friend.

Her cheeks flushed a soft rose color as she lowered her lids and withdrew her hand. He immediately missed the warmth. Uncertainty reflected in her eyes.

Alex glanced at his watch. "Right on time. Remember, the main players in the room want Wycliffe Avenue more than you. If there's something you don't understand, look to me. If I can't readily answer, we'll get the information to them later."

Alex and Lauren exited his car and walked toward the mayor's office located in the tall brick government building on the corner of the square. He pushed opened the door and allowed Lauren to enter first.

Before entering the lobby, he and Lauren went through metal detectors, then took the elevator to the third floor and stepped to the counter.

Alex said, "Lauren Drake and Alex Charland for Mayor Lane."

The young man behind the desk pointed right. "Take the hall to the right, and about halfway down, you'll see a glass-enclosed conference room on the left. They're waiting for you."

"Thanks." Alex nodded to Lauren as they made their way into the meeting room. His mouth dropped open when he saw Mason Williams sitting in one of the chairs.

Lauren stepped up to the table and looked at each person. Then she glared at Mason. "I'm afraid there's been some miscommunication. Mr. Williams is not a part of the Wycliffe Avenue project."

Mason started to interrupt, and Lauren shot him down. "Mason, Bratten purchased the land for the new development from our funds. He set up a separate entity to oversee the Wycliffe Avenue project, which has nothing to do with Drake Properties. And for the record, I have assumed his position at Drake Properties too." Her back straightened, and her chest rose up and down. "Mayor, gentlemen, I am sorry to have wasted your time, but I will not discuss my husband's plans with Mason in the room."

Alex was stunned as the air left the room.

Lauren exuded confidence as she lifted her chin.

Mason stood from the table. The muscles in his jaw worked double time. He glanced away from Lauren, turning to the mayor. "While Mrs. Drake has noble intentions of continuing her husband's legacy, I'd like to remind all parties she has no practical experience in developing a project of this magnitude."

Alex interjected, "I have decades of experience, and I've signed on as CFO to facilitate the project. Since Mason doesn't legally own any of the land proposed for the development, I feel it's unproductive to continue the meeting."

Mason grabbed his iPad and briefcase. "Lauren, I'll speak with you at the office. Charland." And he stormed out of the room.

Mayor Lane exhaled, withdrew a handkerchief from his coat pocket, and patted his forehead. With an exaggerated Southern drawl, he said, "A most ostentatious man that Mason Williams. We thought you invited him to the meeting, Alex."

Riley Gates leaned back in his chair. "Mrs. Drake, please join us at the table, and let's get the ball rolling on the project. We'd like to go over the details to place it on the next council meeting docket."

Brady Weber and Rick Kirkland chimed in unison, "Here, here."

Lauren released a breath, and Alex pulled out the chair for her. She smiled at him and sat down. "Again, my apologies, but Bratten specifically purchased the land with our private funds.

He grew up in your town, and I have his vision for Wycliffe Avenue in my files. Do you have a projector available?"

Mayor Lane said, "Yes, I'll set it up for you."

After the meeting, Lauren and Alex stepped back into the elevator. She did a quick fist pump and hugged Alex's neck on impulse. His arms wrapped around her waist tightly as he lifted her feet off the floor. She inhaled his clean yet masculine scent, and as he eased her feet to the ground, his hand rested on her low back.

She stared back into his grass-green eyes for a few seconds longer than she intended to before taking a step back.

He grinned. "Let's celebrate. Ma Bailey's Diner and Baked Goods is a couple of blocks down. Best lasagna in the county."

The elevator slid open. "All right, that sounds good. Do you think I did okay? They seemed on board with the project."

He dipped his chin slightly. "Good, girl, you did great. We'll have all their questions answered before the city council meeting. Hey, after we eat, I thought we could drive up to the property. I brought my Canon. Bratten loved taking photos during each phase of development."

"Do you think he'd be happy about me taking over the project?"

"Oh, honey, he's smiling down from heaven."

The property Bratten bought was spectacular. Lauren tried to imagine Bratten's design for the development. His ability to orchestrate a project from the beginning to the end was like a great symphony conductor.

Lauren had seen other projects through the different phases from start to finish. Still, Bratten's artist rendering of Wycliffe Avenue created and embodied the city's character, with a luxury hotel, a golf course, high-end shops, and art galleries.

Bratten's vision created a community of homes and condos with a wide range of interior and exterior styles, weaving a plan of beauty.

Could she fill his shoes?

Bratten wanted to encourage pedestrian or bicycle traffic connecting to the downtown square through the trailheads using the existing greenways. He didn't want to level trees and recreate greenery. Bratten wanted to design the project with the current landscape in mind.

He had a list of urban planners and architects bidding on the project. Some of the designs on his computer blew her away, and Lauren revealed the best ones to the spearhead committee.

She crossed her arms over her chest, visualizing the final product. Wycliffe Avenue would be the balm to her wound. It would help her stay connected to Bratten. "Can you see it, Alex?"

"Yes, I can see it. Bratten was a genius. He had a gift few developers ever achieved. Instead of squeezing out every inch of land, he allows for more space. Kinda like the fifties, don't you think?"

Lauren leaned against the hood of Alex's car. "Yeah, that's exactly it. The fifties that some movies and TV shows modeled as the perfect place to live."

Alex leaned next to her and nudged her shoulder. "Small town niche presents a unique opportunity."

Alex was thinking similar thoughts. She understood why Bratten loved him so much.

"In the meeting, you said you're my CFO, so you're going to help me?"

"Yes, ma'am. Eron said he'd line up local contractors and subs. It was Bratten's last dream. Of course, I'm helping you."

"I pissed Mason off. How did he know about the meeting? I didn't tell anyone. Did you?"

"I was wondering the same thing."

Lauren looked up into his eyes with trust, and something happened unexpectedly.

He leaned in close, cupped her face, and searched her eyes, nose, and mouth, but kissing her would ruin everything. She closed her eyes, and he kissed her forehead. "Open your eyes."

She did and sighed relief.

"I am here. I don't intend on going anywhere." He gave her a sideways grin. "Get in the car, Gidget."

"Gidget? As in Sandra Dee's Gidget or Sally Fields?" She chuckled. "I had no idea people still watched old movies and TV shows like I do. It's one of my hobbies."

He laughed aloud. "I guess you could be Gilligan's, Mary Ann." She gave him a mock elbow to the ribs.

"The first day I've laughed since Bratten died. Why does it make me feel guilty?"

He opened the passenger door for her. "Because Bratten isn't here to laugh with us."

Chapter 4

Eagle Creek

Noxzema ran through the subdivision golf course trails and entered Bratten's house from the backyard. Mason gave him a key and the location of the security cameras. He placed three explosive devices strategically through the house to detonate by remote if he couldn't find Bratten's storage device.

He quickly scanned the living area for typical hiding places, rummaging through the desk drawers in the kitchen, the entertainment center, bookshelves, side tables, and coffee table in the living area. He didn't expect to find the portable server in obvious places but didn't want to backtrack.

Noxzema took extra time searching and retrieved several USBs inside the home office, but none of the storage devices held a terabyte. He moved into the main bedroom when someone screamed and ran toward him, slamming his head with a purse that weighed a ton.

Lauren fought him like a wildcat. He placed her in a chokehold throwing her to the floor, pinning her down while he withdrew a syringe and injected her with diamorphine. Then a second person entered the house. The woman in his arms slumped to the ground. That was when he realized she wasn't Lauren.

Lauren grabbed her purse as Alex stopped the car.

"Want me to come inside with you?" he asked.

"Nah, that's Angeline's car. I'll be okay. Today almost felt normal. The project is a good thing. Thanks, Alex." She squeezed his hand, got out of the car, and ran up the sidewalk.

The door was open, and she yelled out Angeline's name. That's when she noticed someone had burglarized her house. She screamed Angeline's name running through the house and found her on the main bedroom floor.

The intruder crouched at the window, half in and half out, when Lauren grabbed the crystal lamp from the dresser and threw it. Glass shattered above his head as he dropped to the ground. Dusk made him near invisible when he hit the tree line to the trails.

Lauren ran back to Angeline.

Alex shouted, "Where are you?"

"In here." Lauren glanced at her broken dresser mirror inside the main bedroom. Her jewelry boxes turned over with the contents strewn about the room. She rubbed Angeline's sternum. "Call 9-1-1. Someone injected her. The syringe is on the floor. The intruder jumped out of the window." She checked Angeline's airways, then proceeded to give her CPR.

Alex called 9-1-1, and within minutes, the first responders pounded the door. He let them in. "We're in the back!"

Paramedics rushed in and took over while Lauren rapidly relayed the events. Still unconscious, Angeline started breathing normally. They placed her on the gurney and took her in the ambulance to the hospital while the police officers questioned Lauren.

Alex handed one of them Detective Stone's business card. His teeth clenched as he threw up a hand. "You may want to call Detective Stone. The person responsible for this jumped out the window. They could still be in the neighborhood."

One of the police officers radioed in the incident and requested backup to search the area.

Lauren squeezed Alex's hand and looked at the other officer. "Is it okay to call Angeline's husband?"

The officer nodded as he took notes. "Yes, but you'll need to stay on the premises. Detective Stone is on the way. He wants to speak with you while we secure the area and gather evidence."

Alex glanced at Lauren. His eyes flashed something raw and dark, almost feral.

She shivered in fear or shock, maybe both, leaning against Alex. He drew her into his arms and didn't let her go until Detective Stone walked through the front door.

Lauren relayed the information about what happened in the house while Alex explained the earlier events with Mason at the Wycliffe meeting.

Detective Stone said, "Mrs. Drake, do you remember anything about the perpetrator beyond the black clothing?"

Lauren blanched.

Was he short or tall, thin or fat?

Her voice was tense, "The door was opened, and my house trashed. I have security cameras. It happened so fast. I was more worried about my sister. Honestly, I can't remember their body type. They were crouched, so not fat, muscular but lean Then, wearing black, it's hard to remember any distinctive qualities." She closed her eyes, trying to remember. Her words seemed inadequate. "Brown eyes, definitely dark brown eyes."

Detective Stone said, "I still have the security company's contact from Bratten's death. I'll give them a call."

She bit her lip to control her anger. "I went to Bratten's office last night. I told Rose I was going to be her boss. I yelled at Mason this morning. I don't think that's a coincidence, do you?"

Detective Stone listened and waited before speaking. "We can't speculate, only investigate and see if either have alibis." He looked at Alex and then back to Lauren. "I wouldn't recommend Mrs. Drake staying in the house. Do you have somewhere to go?"

She looked up at Alex and asked, "Can I stay with you?"

"Of course, you can."

Lauren asked, "Detective, may I go to my room and pack some things?"

Detective Stone's eyes locked with Lauren's. "Processing a crime scene takes time. Please allow my team to do their job. Mrs. Drake, you may want to call your family. The news crews just pulled outside."

"I've already called my family." She hugged herself.

Detective Stone received a text, and his eyelids flickered. "I'm going to get an update from the team leader."

Lauren nervously wrung her hands. Crimes like this happened to other people and not in upscale suburbia. Bratten's murder left her fragile, but the attack on Angeline and the home invasion made her mad and unstable.

Alex joined Lauren at the window. "Do you have any tea?"

"I think so."

They went into the kitchen.

Lauren rummaged into the cupboard and pulled out a variety of teabags. Her hands trembled.

He said, "I'll make it."

Lauren gripped the lip of the counter while Alex made tea.

She whispered, "They have to find DNA this time that'll lead to a suspect. Three weeks have passed since Bratten's murder with no arrests. Whoever killed him was looking for something in my home. I'm not a detective but look at my house...they trashed the place. The syringe. The anonymous letter. Something. I don't see shades of gray only black and white. Mason is involved. I know it. Unless Bratten led a secret life."

He cupped her hands with his. "I promise if Bratten led a secret life, he didn't tell me either. We're going to catch who did this."

"When? Who else will die?" She wanted to yank her hair out. She wondered what Bratten would do. What would Bratten say? Bratten never stumbled. He was always steadfast and sure.

"I need to get my things and go to the hospital."

"When Detective Stone gives us the green light, we'll pack up your things, and you can follow me to my house. We'll park your car in my garage. Then I'll drive us to the hospital to check on Angeline. Deal?"

"I'm too mad to cry. I'm on the verge of falling completely apart, crumbling into pieces. I don't understand why someone is deliberately hurting my family."

Alex's hands shook so badly that he had to place the cup on the counter. "I'm not going to sit around and wait for the authorities to figure it out." His voice lowered as he draped an arm around Lauren's shoulder and hugged her close. "I got you."

"Are you sure you don't mind me staying with you for a few days?"

Alex took a step back while holding onto her biceps. "Of course, I don't mind. It's not safe at your house anymore."

"But how do you know the killer won't come after me at your house? We have a security system, and it didn't go off."

"Besides having a state-of-the-art security system, I live in a gated community with security guards. Someone may get to us, but they'll have a harder time doing it. I'm turning over some of my cases to my partners at the firm. I want to be there for you, and I'm not good at splitting my time."

Reaching for his hand, she said, "I can't ask you to do that for me."

"You're not asking. It's a done deal."

"Wonder what they were looking for?"

He shrugged. "Not sure."

An hour or so later, the police team began to leave Lauren's house, chattering among themselves, barely glancing at her.

Detective Stone stepped back into the living area. "Mrs. Drake, it's okay for you to pack some things."

"I'll be at Alex's for a few days," said Lauren.

Detective Stone glanced at Alex and back to Lauren. With a raised brow, he asked, "The last time we spoke, you mentioned the Wycliffe development. Can you stop by the station tomorrow to give me the details?"

Lauren had regained some of her composure, straightened her back, and lifted her chin. "Detective Stone, please call me Lauren, and I can do better than that. I have the files uploaded to Dropbox. I'll add your email address to the shared folder. Once you have read the files, please call me if you have any questions. Keep me updated on your findings."

Alex seemed in deep thought with his lips firmly pressed together. He crossed his arms over his chest. "Detective Stone, do you have any thoughts on who killed Bratten? Any idea who broke into the house?"

Detective Stone tensed. "I can't comment regarding an ongoing investigation, but I'd appreciate any information to advance our efforts if you come up with anything else." He turned to Alex and said, "I'm aware that Logan Clarkson is on your payroll. He's an excellent investigator." He gave a slight nod and left the house.

"Alex, will you go with me into my bedroom while I gather my things? I'm still shaking."

"Sure."

Lauren stepped into the walk-in closet flipping on the light switch. Reaching up on tiptoe, she pulled a couple of her travel bags off the shelf and began to select a variety of clothes and her credentials for the next few days. She packed both hers and Bratten's laptops into her brief bag.

Alex grabbed her suitcases, and they walked through the house.

She stopped and looked at her wedding photos on the wall. Grief weighed her down with every step.

In the garage, Alex helped her load her things into the back of her SUV. She hit the remote, and prickles raised the hair on her skin. There was a rustle near her crape myrtles too heavy for a cat or dog. Someone was watching them. Her stomach dipped in fear.

Alex scanned the landscaping as he placed his hand on the vehicle's roof. "Someone's out there. Get in the car and buckle up. Call me, and we'll talk on the way to my house."

Lauren watched him as he walked down the drive, slid into his car, and backed out onto the street, waiting for her. She followed Alex about two car links behind. Her eyes widened nervously, glancing into the rearview mirror. Her breaths were ragged, her heart pounding, and the air in her lungs constricted as she neared the end of her street.

A sonic boom reverberated louder than any thunder she'd ever heard. She glanced back, and the evening sky lit up with an orange fireball that was her house. She spun the car in the middle of the road, squealing tires as she slammed the gas.

Pulling across the street, Lauren watched helplessly as flames shot out her house windows and doors, shooting nails and broken glass into the air and raining down shrapnel. Dazed, she got out of her car. Everything that she and Bratten had built together went up in flames. More explosions blew chunks of the wood and brick projectiles as Lauren covered her head from the falling debris.

Earlier today's tiny spark of hope turned into searing pain as thick plumes of smoke billowed into the sky. Despair turned into anger, and anger turned to rage. The putrid stench of smoke made her gag. The fire department and police sirens drowned out her cries.

Lauren fell hard to her knees as the last remnants of her life with Bratten disappeared like sand sifting through an hourglass. Her white-knuckled fists pounded the ground. Hatred toward those responsible burned down on her like acid rain. Her emotions boiled over into pieces of molten anguish.

Alex came up behind Lauren and pulled her from the ground. She kicked, screamed, and clawed as he carried her away from the devastation that was now her life. He said something, but Lauren couldn't hear him. A whirlwind of dread overcame her conscious thoughts, and she faded into the black, and darkness swallowed her whole.

Alex headed toward the emergency room but changed his mind midway and drove to his house only a few minutes from Lauren's. He stopped at the gate long enough for the guard to recognize him, then went into the subdivision.

Gripping the steering wheel, Alex cursed under his breath. Hatred spread and consumed his soul.

Vengeance!

Destruction for those responsible for taking the love and light out of Lauren's eyes. He looked at her, slumped in the passenger seat, and remembered what his grandmother said before she died, *"Hate smothers the soul and leaves no room for love, joy or happiness."*

Torn by conflicting emotions, Alex would kill to see her smile again. The light in her eyes danced this afternoon as she created an image of Bratten's last project. Only to come home and find her world annihilated. The light in her eyes turned to rage.

No, Alex would help pave the road to her recovery with love. That didn't mean he intended to roll over and play dead. Nope. Alex knew how to fight. He'd learned the hard way.

At twelve, Alex was alone in the world. His grandmother had died, and the state had placed him in a boys' home. He had to learn to fight to survive. Darwin didn't have anything on him. He'd learned the "survival of the fittest" firsthand, and he had the scars to prove it.

It was the love his grandmother had given him. Her life lessons and unconditional love helped him weather the storm from his share of beatings from the students and the teachers. He could've turned to a life of crime but instead chose to learn the criminal justice system. He studied hard and made good grades. Through his excellent fortune, he applied to Wycliffe College and roomed with Bratten Drake.

Bratten and his Aunt Lynda soothed the savage beast that raged in him from his adolescence, and when he graduated law school with honors, he used Bratten's connections to close Howard's School for Boys. With Bratten's help, Alex set up a scholarship for orphans. He set up workshops and groups to help troubled teens.

Bratten's death and the terror tactics from the past couple of days had him on edge. He searched into local organized crime the day Bratten died. The explosion tonight was another indicator that more than one person was involved. He didn't know who Bratten had gotten involved with, but one of them was Mason Williams.

Alex intended to use his legal prowess to destroy everyone involved in Bratten's death. He drove down two streets, turning onto Riverside Trail. Five houses down on the right, Alex pulled into the driveway of his three-level contemporary home.

He'd called Detective Stone to inform him, but people heard the explosion for miles. Ray was at the scene with Logan Clarkson.

He pressed the remote and pulled his SUV into the garage next to the silver Jeep. The garage door slid shut. Alex got out of the vehicle and went to the passenger door, scooping Lauren in his arms.

Her head rested against his neck. He brought her into the house up to the second floor into the guest bedroom and placed her on the bed. She rolled away from him, curling up into a ball. He put his hand softly on her back.

"I've lost everything. Alex, go away. Leave me alone."

"No, I'm not going anywhere. Do you hear me, Lauren?"

She rolled back over and looked up at him. Her face was wet with tears. "Why is this happening?"

"I wish I had the answers, but I don't. I promise I won't stop until someone pays." His fingers fanned her hair across the pillow.

"Will you hand me my purse? I want to check on Angeline."

"It's in the truck. I'll be right back. Do you want a cup of tea? A drink?"

"Tea, please." She said, "I'm going to kill the person responsible for destroying my life."

Alex didn't say anything. The anger welled up inside of him. He wanted to kill whoever did this too.

Lauren looked around at the rustic touches mixed with contemporary elements in the room. The bed had a black head and footboard with a white duvet. The plush carpet and walls had a mixture of grays, blacks, browns, and whites.

She sat up in bed when Alex returned with her purse and a cup of chai tea. "The room's lovely, Alex."

He handed her the purse and placed the tea on the nightstand. "Not me, my designer. She asked me what colors I liked, and she ran with it." He placed her packed bags in a closet with what resembled a sliding barn door.

"I'll unpack later. I want to call the hospital and check on Angeline." Her phone buzzed. "Lauren Drake." She pressed on the phone speaker.

Detective Stone said, "Lauren, I wanted to check on you."

"Me? Why? Because someone blew up my house? Someone killed my husband, and what have you done? Nothing. Not a damn thing."

Alex took the phone from her. "Detective, Lauren is distraught. We know you're doing your best."

"I don't blame Lauren for being angry. I'm angry more than you know. I also checked with the hospital and posted an officer at Angeline's door. I thought you'd want to know she's in a room on the third floor. Room 3106. I'll stop by and talk to her tomorrow."

"Thank you, Detective," said Alex.

"Gotcha. I'll talk to you later." He hung up.

Lauren sat on the edge of the bed. "Someone came for me and found my sister."

"Yeah, that's what I think too. Logan left me a message. He's coming over here tomorrow afternoon. Angeline is in a room, and she's sleeping. Do you want to call her?"

"Not if she's sleeping. I'll text Eron."

Lauren: I'm at Alex's. How's sister?

Eron: She's shaken up pretty good but sleeping. I saw on the news about your house. I'm sorry.

Lauren: Me too. I feel like someone's suckered punched me. Have you heard from Mom and Dad?

Eron: Yes, They're worried. And they have a right to be. Want me to let them know you're okay? I figure you may not be up to it.

Lauren: That would be awesome. Call me if she needs me.

Eron: Get some rest. You're going to need it.

Lauren: Don't I know it.

Lauren ran through the woods. Limbs and branches cut into her skin. Someone dressed in black chased her. He wanted her dead. She tripped and slid down a steep embankment. The man straddled her, wrapped his hands around her throat, and choked her.

She fought, kicking and clawing.

Lauren woke abruptly, out of breath, heart racing, and wringing wet with sweat.

It took Lauren a few minutes to register she was at Alex's house. The moonlight lit the room. She rolled onto her side, propped on her elbow. She heard Alex snoring in the next room, well, more of a rattle.

Alex had been so kind to her. His expressive green eyes changed hues based on his moods. He was worried, and so was she.

It was still too hard to think of Bratten as deceased. Their home burned. She closed her eyes and saw him vividly in her mind's eye.

Bratten. If you can see me in heaven, give me a sign. Let me know if you're okay. I love you. I miss you.

Her heart thumped unsteadily as her belly dipped with longing. She needed someone to hold her, not a sexual need but a physical need.

Lauren wondered what it would be like to lie in Alex's arms with her head on his chest. She thought about the rhythm of Alex's beating heart. The blood still coursing through his veins.

She'd taken Bratten's heartbeat for granted and her life with him, what she wouldn't give to hear Bratten's heartbeat just one more time.

Logan stared at the flames turning to embers destroying Drake's million-dollar home. Bombers didn't care who they killed, but Lauren was still alive for some reason. One theory rolled around his brain that the perpetrator searched the house for something incriminating in Bratten's death and didn't find it.

After the fire department extinguished the flames, the acrid chemical smell lingered in the air. Bomb technicians worked for hours as the local officers evacuated a two-block radius if another device detonated.

The feds arrived on the scene, worked with the local authorities to secure the area, and interviewed the rubberneckers.

He stayed out of the way but briefly spoke to one of his forces contacts as the news crews went live on Chief Willard Lee.

Camera lights glared on the chief as dawn approached.

Chief Willard didn't need a mic. His voice carried throughout the crime scene. "The Eagle Creek Police Department worked with federal agencies to evacuate the neighborhood due to an explosion at 2552 Meadowview Lane. Bomb technicians cleared the house and cross-referenced the evidence to ensure our citizens' safety before those families returned home."

He looked to each of the cameras and continued, "With a high degree of certainty, we believe the bombing is an isolated incident and may relate to the recent murder of Bratten Drake. The tedious process of identifying the source of the explosion is ongoing. Our officers, along with the federal agencies, are canvassing the area. Please visit the Eagle Creek Police Department's website."

The reporters shouted a rush of questions, and the chief threw up his hand. "Thank you." He turned and melted among the other officers behind the yellow tape to protect the crime scene, the officers, and the onlookers.

Detective Ray Stone stepped over to Logan. "Technically, you're not supposed to be here."

Logan shoved his hands into his jean pockets. "Yeah, but I'm here. From the smell: dynamite, let me guess, and I bet you found timing device mechanisms controlled remotely, which indicates the bomber has experience. Military or someone who uses dynamite to clear job sites like Drake Properties?"

Ray shook his head. "You got it all figured out, Ace. Why don't you come work for us, and our jobs will be much easier?"

"Tsk, tsk. That's not an answer, but I'll take it my theory is ringing close to the truth."

Chief Lee looked at Logan and scowled.

"I guess that's my cue to skedaddle. I'll share mine if you share yours."

Ray growled. "Get lost, Logan, before the chief has our heads."

Logan entered a few notes on his mobile. His contact with the force sent him a text:

Witness saw the bomber, dressed from head to toe in black, running on the cart trails, racing toward the golf house. My guess is he's long gone by now. Oh, Mason Williams has an airtight alibi.

Logan slowly walked to his truck. Mason may have had an alibi, but that didn't mean he wasn't involved. Lauren or Alex may have the contact info of the person responsible for excavating land that works for Drake Properties. He was getting close to the answers. He could feel it.

Six-thirty the following day, Mason stormed into The Dirty Rat's back room. "What the hell happened, man?"

Noxzema sat hunched over with his hands on the chair. "How'd I know her sister would show up? The first thing I did was wire the place to blow if I didn't find Bratten's storage device. Do you see his server? Ah, hell no. There were a couple of USBs, and Bratten's laptop wasn't in the office. I blew the house in case his server was still in there."

"You're a complete moron. The feds are involved now. Did anyone tell you to blow the place? Geesh, Noxzema, we could've contained the investigation locally, but guess who'll be the number one suspect—ME!" He slammed his fist into Noxzema's pretty face.

The Colonel blew into the room like the freaking Tasmanian Devil. "Break it up, ladies. Have you lost your mind? This stops now. I'll handle the feds. Mason, you handle the locals." He turned to Noxzema and shouted, "If you were going to torch the place, why didn't you do it with her in it? For crying out loud, do I have to do everything around here? Until you get the okay from me, no one touches the widow. Everyone must lay low until the feds leave. *Capiche?*"

T-bone and Mole strolled into the room looking like death on a cracker.

The Colonel whipped around to Mason. "Then when the insurance money comes in, kill the widow and Charland. Make it look like an accident. T-bone, you contact Esteban. We may need his help later. Get it together, people. I haven't worked for this long, this hard to end up in prison." He left as fast as he came in.

Mason left, grumbling under his breath. He'd used the legitimacy of Drake Properties to mask the true nature of the RB's interests allowing them to trade illegal arms and transfer large sums of money to offshore accounts untraceable by the government. Each brother had a legitimate job; each brother played an integral part in keeping the well-oiled RB machine running.

Mason had remained in the shadows until Bratten wanted to squeeze him out of Drake Properties. He recalled the evening.

"Mason, do you have a few minutes to talk?"

"Sure, man. Pull up a chair. I'm trying to finish the Hall's Haven plat." Mason closed his laptop. "What's up?"

Bratten crossed one leg over the other, his right elbow on the armrest. "I've decided to dissolve Drake Properties. I want to move back to my hometown of Wycliffe and set up a new office. It has nothing to do with your caliber of work. I have an opportunity to help the town that helped me. I'm telling Lauren tonight. I think it's best to dissolve the LLC, I trust, amicably. I'm also working on getting green cards for all of our migrant workers through legal channels."

Mason's blood roared through his veins. It had taken an enormous amount of his time to set up the front with Drake Properties. Bratten was a respectable member of the community. No one would ever suspect him or his business to be involved with anything illegal. Mason wasn't about to walk away from his gravy train. "Bratten, dude, why can't you keep this office open and branch out to the new location in Wycliffe? And I told you I had the green card situation under control."

Bratten raised a brow, pressed his lips firmly together, and shifted in his seat. "I've had Alex file paperwork in Wycliffe to establish a sole proprietorship. While I've enjoyed our time working together, I'm moving in a new direction, and you should too. We can talk with our employees, contractors, subs, and vendors. You've built a solid reputation and should have no problem branching out on your own."

Mason narrowed his eyes and clenched his right fist. "I don't want to dissolve the LLC. I have no desire to dissolve it. I say you rethink your decision." He threw his hands up, palms out.

"Why mess up a good thing, Bratten? Why should things get nasty?"

It irritated Mason how Bratten Drake never seemed agitated and kept his calm in nearly every situation.

Bratten casually rose from the chair and placed his fingertips on Mason's desk. He leaned in and said, "I'm moving on with or without you on board. I don't think you want to play hardball with me."

Mason stood and glared at Bratten. "You have no idea who you're messing with, Bratten Drake. Rethink your decision. Once the games begin, I don't stop until I win."

He remembered how cool Bratten was when he walked out of his office with his back straight and shoulders back. If the damn smug bastard had just left well enough alone, but no, Bratten had morals. Mason left his morals on the battlefields in the Middle East with Andre.

Andre Rossi had been his best friend, and he had morals too. His death was deemed from friendly fire. Southern Security in the Middle East didn't offer their recruits any long-term employee benefits like the military. It was one of the leading reasons the RB formed.

Andre, the poor bastard, didn't have a chance.

Andre came into the barracks and threw his gear on the bed. "Mason, I'm getting out. Rose is pregnant. I can't continue as a contract killer, and don't look at me like that. You know, I call a spade a spade. As soon as my contract's up, I'm outta here."

Mason grimaced. "The Colonel will never let you leave. You know too much."

"The Colonel can kiss my hairy ass. I'm going to be a dad. Rosie and my child are the only things that matter to me."

Mason looked over his shoulder, and the Colonel glared at Andre. "Lock and load, girls. We have a mission."

The next day, Andre was dead.

Chapter 5

The morning light streamed into Alex's bedroom, but he'd been up for an hour before the sunrise. He couldn't sleep. The vivid images of Bratten's house in flames and Lauren's expression of despair tugged at his heartstrings. Pandemonium broke loose, and all he could do was bring Lauren home.

Danger seemed to lurk at every corner.

Alex slipped into the guest room to check on Lauren. He didn't want to wake her. Alex watched her sleep for a few minutes. She grieved her lost love, her home, and Alex was the closest to Bratten left.

The flowery scent of Lauren's hair filled his brain as the pale sunlight moved across her skin like the delicate petals of a pink rose.

The thing about Bratten was he knew how Alex felt about Lauren, and he still loved him anyway. Bratten didn't have a jealous bone in his body. He was a one in a million kind of guy because he wouldn't have been so gracious if the shoe had been on the other foot.

Decisions, good or bad, always yield consequences. Bratten must've made a wrong turn on his journey in life.

Ugh, life wasn't fair to take Bratten from Lauren or him.

Alex glanced at his watch and then covered Lauren with a blanket. He slipped out of the room and went for a run. Forty-five minutes later, he showered, shaved, and dressed for his eight o'clock meeting.

Inside the kitchen, he pulled out a drawer and grabbed a notepad.

Lauren,

I hope you slept well. Early meeting today, but I'll be back by two. Logan is coming here at three to discuss his findings. I'm leaving you the keys to the Jeep to drive. One of Logan's team members left your car at my office last night. We can pick it up later.

Call me if you need anything,

Alex

Lauren woke to the sound of a door closing. She opened her eyes and found a note on the nightstand from Alex and read it. Grabbing her purse off the floor, Lauren reached for her phone. She'd missed two calls from Eron, so he left her a text.

Eron: Angeline is released. Heading home. She said not to worry about her, to worry about yourself.

Lauren: Tell her that's easier said than done. I'll stop by your house in an hour or so with pastries.

Eron: We're home. Already had breakfast. She's sleeping. Why don't you stop by tomorrow when the kids come back?

Lauren: Okay. I read you loud and clear, Papa Bear. I'll leave her alone today.

Eron: Be careful, sister. Someone wants your head.

Lauren: No worries. I have the Hatter. Hey, would you consider working with Drake Properties? You don't have

to work in the office. You can work from your house. I need someone I can trust.

Eron: Let me talk with your sister. You know, she's the boss.

Lauren: Yeah, I've known that most of my life. Love you.

Eron: Love you more.

Lauren stepped into the walk-in closet. She opened the suitcases, hung her clothes, and placed her toiletries in the bathroom.

The fire had destroyed most of her clothes and shoes. But she couldn't dwell on everything she'd lost. She'd worry about that later.

She jumped into the shower and allowed the hot water to rain down for several minutes before washing her hair and body.

After dressing, Lauren called Drake Properties, and Amber, the receptionist, answered. Lauren said, "Good morning, Amber. Would you put me through to Rose?"

"Good morning, Mrs. Drake. Rose isn't in. May I help you?"

Where was she? "Did Rose say what time she'd be in?"

"No, ma'am, but Mr. Williams is in the office. Would you like to speak to him?"

"Amber, does Bratten have any messages this morning? I'm trying to follow up on any business transactions."

"No, Mrs. Drake. I'm so sorry about your beautiful home. Oh, Mr. Williams had all of Mr. Drake's calls redirected to him after...." Amber stopped talking.

Lauren heard sniffles. "It's okay, Amber. From now on, if anyone calls for Bratten, give them my number. It's in the system. I want to have an employee meeting on Monday. I'm taking over Bratten's position at the company. I'll draft an email and send it out later today. I want to assure everyone that Drake Properties is secure. Bratten cared about every one of you."

More sniffles. "Yes, ma'am."

Lauren jogged down the stairs.

She hadn't noticed her surroundings last night. Alex kept a neat house. She loved the warm interiors, rock walls, vaulted ceilings, and custom lighting, and he had an ultracool kitchen.

She rambled through the cabinets and pantry for coffee. "Ugh, only tea," she sighed. She needed java. She'd stop for coffee on the way to The Flower Shoppe. She'd called in a new arrangement for Bratten's grave.

She grabbed Alex's Jeep key and one of his ballcaps and went into the garage. She got in the vehicle, clicked the remote garage door opener, and backed out of the drive.

After leaving the subdivision gate, Lauren looked both ways, then took a right onto the highway. She pulled around to Drink A Bean's drive-through and ordered a large coffee with sugar in the raw and cream. Then made her way to pick up the arrangement.

Lauren wanted to clean away the lawn clippings around Bratten's grave and see if his headstone had arrived. She needed to talk to Bratten about everything. She just wanted to be near him.

Walking up the steep incline of the cemetery, Lauren noticed Bratten's headstone, then clutched her throat sucking in a deep breath. A man stood with his back to her, someone that looked like...

The man turned slowly to face her, and she met his crystal blue eyes as a slight curve crept into his lips— she fainted.

Lauren didn't know how long she lay on the ground, but when she got the nerve to open her eyes, Alex stared at her with Bratten's blue eyes.

Lauren had finally gone off the deep end of the pond.

She whispered breathlessly, "Bratten."

He knelt on the ground without touching her. "It's me, Lauren."

"How is that possible in Alex's body?" She pointed to his headstone and stammered, "You're, you're...."

"Dead. I can still finish your sentences."

She'd heard of bereavement hallucinations and shook her head. "This isn't real. You're not real."

He said, "I don't have much time. I made big mistakes. I'd never put you in danger intentionally. You know that, right?"

Lauren bit her lip as she edged closer to the hallucination. "You're an illusion brought on by stress. You're not real but a figment of my imagination."

She timidly reached out to touch him, and Alex leaned back on his heels, blinked, and Bratten's blue eyes turned green.

She frowned and sat on the edge of the headstone. "You-you had blue eyes."

Alex stared at her. "What happened? I stopped by to check on his headstone and blanked."

She stammered, "You-you said you were Bratten. You sounded like him too."

Lauren rubbed her forehead and her eyes. "Did I imagine it?" She sunk to her knees beside him. She touched the side of his face.

Alex said, "I-I don't know. I was standing staring at the headstone, and then I was gone, but not gone. It felt like a dream, you know. Maybe, it was Bratten."

Lauren sighed. "Do you believe that?"

Alex nodded. "Why not? If it happens again, ask me something only you and Bratten would know. If I answer correctly, maybe our conscious minds are as open as our unconscious ones. I mean, I talk to my grandmother in my dreams."

It was as if a ton of pressure lifted from her weary soul. She didn't question her sanity. She didn't want to.

Alex blinked again, and Bratten was back. She wasn't frightened but at ease with him, as if he'd never left.

Looking into Bratten's eyes, she said, "Did you know someone tried to kill Angeline? Someone blew up our house. I think whoever killed you wants me dead too. I was so scared last night."

"Oh, my god." He clenched and unclenched his fists. "I can't remember who killed me. But I do remember some things. I did illegal things while I was alive, Lauren. I tried to rationalize my decisions, but it was wrong. So, I thought the best thing was to move us away."

"And they killed you. What did you do?"

"I smuggled illegals over the border. Well, not me, personally, but I paid for it. Mason talked me into doing it. I knew it was wrong, but he convinced me that they would have a better life here. That their families could come later, but in the long run, Mason lied. He works them like indentured servants. I'm responsible. I agreed."

"Do you remember if it was Mason that killed you?"

"I remember the suite at The Hamilton. You and I made love, and we fell asleep. I woke up thirsty, and the little fridge in the room only had sodas, so I put on my sweats and went to the vending room for a couple of water bottles. The next thing I remember was a pain in my stomach. Terrible pain. You were screaming, and then my chest felt like it was on fire."

Lauren hugged him tightly. "Oh, honey. I remember the look of pain on your face. I felt helpless."

He released her embrace and entwined his fingers with hers. "Then I was in the white room. I felt fine, better than fine. I felt an overpowering sense of love. My mom and aunt, whom I hadn't seen in years, were there. Holding me, and we melted from the room into the cottage." He pointed to her. "You and Angeline were there. You said you felt me. It's so weird, Lauren. When you left the cottage, I lost you until now."

"Where is Alex?"

He turned and seemed puzzled then Alex's green eyes stared back at her. "It happened again?"

"Yes." Her eyes went wide.

Alex laughed. "It was Bratten. I heard him. It's like I'm sleepwalking. Or dreaming awake. Like watching a dream, you know, you're not really in it."

"Isn't that fantastic? Oh, Alex, he's back." She reached over and caressed his face with the palms of her hands. "I can't believe this is happening."

"I believe in everything." Alex said, "But Logan is due at my house. We better leave."

She stood and held out her hand. Her breath caught as he leaned in and kissed the side of her neck, sending shivers up her spine. She glanced into the deep blue eyes and sighed.

Bratten used Alex's body. "I miss you, Lauren. I had to find you. Mom and Aunt Lynda argued with me. They said it's against the rules, and I may cause you more pain. I never want to hurt you. I love you so much still."

Part of Lauren wanted to stay in the same spot and not move. Afraid Bratten would disappear. Afraid she'd imagined it all. "Kiss me, Bratten."

The air around them stilled. Time suspended. Bratten didn't move, neither did she until he slipped his hand around the nape of her neck and pulled her to him. He covered her mouth with a kiss that sent shockwaves coursing through her body. His lips tasted the same yet so different.

Blood pounded through her veins with the treble of a freight train.

He released a moan, or maybe she did. Her belly dipped as she tangled her fingers in his hair. The adrenaline rush of kissing them both, Bratten and Alex, at the same time was surreal.

Was she imagining, or was it real?

Locked in a make-out session defying the heavens, Lauren's fingers glided over his shoulders and down his back.

She pulled back with kissed swollen lips searching Alex's face, seeing Bratten's blue eyes, and wanting the taste of his lips to linger. No words expressed raw emotions desperate for more as Alex's eyes turned green. A guttural sound emitted from Alex as he slanted his mouth over hers, slipping his tongue deftly between the seams of her lips.

Thoughts swirled frantically in her mind, but Lauren pushed them away as he retracted and brushed his lips against hers. His arms encased her in a longing embrace, and her sadness spilled away into the hope that life never ended.

Alex released his grip, and the look in his green eyes made her question her sanity again. "I won't apologize for kissing you. He started it."

Lauren's cheeks flushed, and she released a giggle. "He sure did, or maybe I did." Her hands withdrew, and she backed down the hill, staring at Alex like she never had before. "I'll meet you back at the house then?"

Alex caught up with Lauren and reached for her hand as they walked to her car in silence, her thoughts running a marathon of questions and possibilities.

He opened the driver's side door, placing his left hand on the roof. "Be safe. I won't be far behind." His eyes searched her face as his thumb softly caressed the back of her hand. "This thing that just happened with Bratten needs to go slow." He swallowed, releasing an audible sigh. "Okay."

Lauren nodded. A pulse of electricity shot through her body. She reached up and touched her lips, remembering the kisses. "Yes, we need to take it slow."

He said, "Buckle up," and walked to his SUV and slid inside, waiting for her to leave.

Alex watched Lauren pull out of the cemetery, his heart still pounding from the experience with Bratten and that kiss. Oh lord, that kiss sent him soaring. He glanced up in the rearview;

Bratten stared back. Alex touched his face. He felt the same, but Bratten's image appeared in the mirror.

You kissed my wife, Bratten said using what Alex thought was telepathy.

With a frown, he replied, "You started it. You kissed Lauren with my lips using my body. What's that about? Huh? I'm nearing a panic attack, so you want to tell me what is happening?"

Bratten stared at him from the mirror. "Don't drive yet because I'm not sure how that will work. Do you know the still small voice that tells you right from wrong? I'm using the same channel to communicate with you, just on different frequencies. It's new to me too. I'm new to the death scene, so I have little patience. I'm going to be quick. Get Lauren and go to Citizen's Bank. Tell her to bring the lockbox key. There's a package that may shed some light on my murder. She's in danger, Alex. Those bastards don't play."

"What bastards? Who? What happened to you?" Alex felt Bratten's presence leave the car.

Those bastards don't play. That's what Bratten had communicated. Bratten must've been in way over his head to get killed, not to mention those same people blowing up Lauren's house.

His hands shook while he pulled into the subdivision. The security guard waved him through the gate.

Alex reached for his mobile and pushed Siri, *Call Logan.*

Siri: Which phone number for Logan Clarkson? Mobile or work?

Alex: Mobile.

Siri: Calling Logan Clarkson's mobile.

Logan answered on the second ring. "Hey, Alex. I was going to call you. Running a bit late today after last night's investigation. I should make your house around three-thirty." Alex replied, "That works for me. I'm driving Lauren to the bank. Logan, do you have any leads besides Mason?"

Logan chuckled. "So, you think it's Mason too. We'll talk later, Alex." He hung up.

Alex parked in the driveway and ran inside the house. Lauren drank a glass of water from the ceramic crock water dispenser in the kitchen. "Do you have a copy of the lockbox key, or was it in your house?"

"It's in my bag with the other credentials I packed before the explosion. Why?" She leaned against the counter, fingering her ponytail.

"Bratten left something in there for us. We need to go to Citizen's Bank. Is your lockbox at the branch downtown or the one on Vine Street?"

"Downtown. Give me a few minutes to change clothes."

He nodded and watched her jog through the living area past the rock fireplace as the sunlight poured through the floor-to-ceiling windows, and she disappeared up the stairs. He went into the bathroom next to the laundry room, splashed cold water on his face, grabbed a hand towel, and wiped off the excess water. His hands rested on the edge of the sink, and he stared into the mirror. Waiting for Bratten to appear.

He didn't.

Lauren's mind whirled.

Whew. That make-out session with Bratten and Alex brought a new twist to her life she certainly didn't expect. She quickly changed clothes, grabbed the key, and raced downstairs.

Looking at Alex, she said, "I'll drive just in case Bratten pops back."

Alex nodded. They slid into the Jeep and drove to the gate.

The guard looked at the clipboard, then handed her license back. "Thank you, Mrs. Drake." He nodded to Alex. "Mr. Charland," he added with a smirk.

Were her thoughts so easily read on her face?

Alex was the vessel for her late husband. And, well, he was a pretty good kisser to boot.

Driving to downtown Eagle Creek, Lauren glanced at Alex, and Bratten's blue eyes stared back at her. "Do you think you could give me a little warning when you do that? You scared me half to death. I thought I imagined you. I seriously think I'm losing my mind."

Bratten explained how the channeling worked. "It's okay, Lauren, to have mixed feelings about the kiss."

"Are you freaking kidding me? The kiss was great, but I'm talking to a dead guy using his best bud's body for communication while we track a killer. I think I have more on my mind than sex."

"Ah, ha! You're thinking about having sex with my best friend."

"Really? Now, you're jealous? Let's focus on the matter at hand. What am I looking for in the lockbox?"

"Inside the lockbox, you'll find a package with an external server. There's a copy of a second set of Drake Properties books in addition to Mason's log regarding smuggling humans across the border. Mason cooked the books, and I think Rose helped him."

She frowned, reached over, and punched his arm. "That's for not telling me you had an affair with Rose. You should've told me."

He tilted his head and smirked. "Did your new boyfriend tell you that?"

"So, help me, Bratten Alan Drake, I'll scream if you try to pin on me the things you've done that wrecked our lives."

Alex's shoulders slumped, and Bratten was gone.

Shaking her head, Lauren sighed. "Looks like both of us are having difficulty grappling with our current situation. I'm sorry for hitting you, Alex. I couldn't help myself. Are you able to hear our conversations?"

"Yes." Alex remained silent until they pulled into the bank parking lot. He said, "We get in and get out, fast. Someone could've followed us. After getting the package, go to my office, and I'll make duplicate copies of whatever is on that device."

"Gotcha."

Lauren approached the vault inside the bank, pressed her hand on the security pad, and keyed in the passcode. Alex followed her in and the vault door sealed behind them. She scanned the wall, searching for their number, then withdrew her key and unlocked the box pulling out the drawer.

The drawer held her jewels, Bratten's mother's and aunt's jewelry, and wrapped cash. She picked up the package and looked inside. "Got it." She took the device out and slipped it into her purse.

Exiting the vault, Alex said, "Let's stop by The Holy Shrimp for a few California rolls."

Lauren rolled her eyes. "Sure, why not?"

They left the bank and got into the vehicle driving fast to Charland and Associates.

"The Holy Shrimp?" she asked.

"I thought it'd sound more casual if someone were listening."

Bratten returned. "Yuck, he still eats that stuff."

Lauren replied, "I'm starving. Sushi is healthy and omega-three-rich."

Bratten placed his hand on her thigh and squeezed. "Yeah, well, eating healthy didn't keep me alive, did it?"

Lauren moved his hand off her leg. "Stop it. I mean it. I won't allow you to take advantage of Alex."

"Oh. I'm not taking advantage of Alex." Bratten adjusted Alex's pants.

Alex blinked several times and shivered. "That's freaking me out. We will have to talk with Bratten about time sharing my body."

Lauren shook her head and pulled into the front parking space at Charland and Associates. "Alex, do you mind if I sit in the Jeep? I'm exhausted and need to close my eyes for a minute."

He squeezed her hand. "No problem. I'll be back soon."

Lauren leaned the seat back and closed her eyes, paying attention to her breathing. She made a mental checklist of practical things that needed her attention.

Planning Monday's meeting at Drake Properties.

The burned-out house.

What was she going to do with their destroyed home?

She had to change her address and purchase replacement items.

Her mobile rang, making her jump. It was Angeline.

"Just checking on you, baby sister. We didn't want to bother you last night. I thought I'd check this afternoon and see if you need Eron and me to work through any damage. See if anything is salvageable."

"No hurry. You need to rest. I called my insurance rep this morning. They're waiting for a police report anyway."

"Do what Alex suggested. Hire a bodyguard. Mom and Dad, all of us are worried sick."

Lauren sighed. "No more than I am. Alex is sort of my bodyguard for the moment. We're meeting with a private investigator this afternoon. I'm going to fight, Angeline. I'm starting Monday with Drake Properties. Hey, gotta go. Got a date with a ghost."

"Lauren, what *are* you talking about?"

"Love you, sis." She ended the call.

Alex hopped in the front seat. "I put one copy in my safe, I made another copy for you, one for Logan, and we'll put the original back in the lockbox."

She said, "Do you mind if I stop by the post office? I need to fill out a change of address form, and after we pick up take-out, I'm stopping by my place to see if we have mail. Bills don't stop coming because of...." She paused.

"Because of Bratten's death? Because someone tried to kill your sister and then blew up your house? It's okay, Lauren. You can speak freely around me. I'm trying to process the events too."

"My life is in shambles."

Alex placed his forearm on the console. "You must redirect that kind of thinking. We're going to beat them. Just keep saying it. I think you should leave your car here for a few days. We lock the gates at night. Oh, you don't have to go to the post office to make a change of address. You can fill the forms out online."

"Sounds like a plan. Alex, do you know a good therapist?"

Alex replied, "I do. I see her once a month. I've been seeing one for years."

"May I ask why?"

Talking about Howard's Boys School was more straightforward than it used to be. He relayed the events in almost a monotone. "Bratten saved my life back then. He and I may not be blood, but we're brothers. I have conflicted emotions about you. I fell in love with you the same time Bratten met you. Do you remember dancing with me at The Swan Ball?"

Her eyes widened, and she gave him a brilliant smile melting his heart. "I do remember. That was before I started dating Bratten, officially. You kissed me."

"I did. You were it for me. That sounds corny. I know it does. I kissed you, and every other girl after paled in comparison."

"Why didn't you tell me?" She turned onto Meadowview Lane.

Alex grabbed his heart in an overly dramatic gesture. "Because the moment Bratten Drake entered the room, I paled in comparison. On a sultry summer night, your face lit up like a full moon, and your starry eyes burned for him, not me. Hey, don't feel sorry for me. I date women. I've dated women. Maybe you were my dream, the girl that got away."

Lauren stopped the car on the street and burst into tears.

Alex held her in his arms, allowing her the time to cry it out.

With ragged breaths, she cried, "Our beautiful home is gone. I don't think I have the strength to sift through the rubble."

He brushed the silky strands from her face and tucked a stray behind her ear. "You can build again."

She shook her head and wiped the tears with her fingers. "No. Once I go through and see if anything is left, I want to level it and sell the lot. I think I may move to Wycliffe."

"The cottage?" Alex asked.

"Oh, no. That'd be too painful. No, I think I'd like to start over with a home in the Wycliffe Avenue community. Once Bratten's killers are brought to justice, I'll dissolve Drake Properties and start over. Is that wishful thinking?"

"Sometimes wishful thinking is the only thing that gets us through the day. Sit here, and I'll check the mailbox." He went to the mailbox, withdrew several letters, and stopped. He glanced up at Lauren and held his breath. She had another anonymous card.

His hands shook as he slid into the passenger seat. He handed her the card.

Lauren's fingers trembled as she opened the envelope and withdrew the mixed collage of letters that formed two sentences: *It doesn't stop here. It won't until you're dead.*

Lauren released a scream that would've shattered crystal.

Alex got out of the Jeep, went around to the driver's side, and pulled her out.

She cried, "I can't take anymore. I can't. I'm going to implode."

Alex held her for a while. He didn't have sufficient words of comfort. He was mad as hell.

She shook loose and shouted, "I'm not taking this shit lying down. We have the server with evidence. That card may have DNA. The stamp could have DNA too. Should we call Detective Stone?"

He shook his head. "I think we should give the card to Logan. Let him run tests, and then he'd give it to the authorities. We have no idea who's involved or how far-reaching. Better to be safe than sorry. Do you want me to drive?"

She shouted, "No. I can drive. I'm sorry, but I'm so mad I could chew up nails and spit out a barbed wire fence."

After parking in his garage, Alex draped an arm around Lauren's shoulder, walking into the house. He lifted her chin and said, "I'm with you, one hundred percent of the way. No matter what the server reveals. No matter the danger. I don't want you to be afraid. Do you trust me?"

"I do trust you, but I trusted Bratten too. He lied to me."

"He omitted some things."

"Don't split hairs with me. An omission is the same as a lie, a spruced-up word masking the truth. Bratten had an affair. He used people. They work for me now, and I want to know who they are and where they live. I won't be a party to anything illegal—no more lies. If you find something out, Alex, you tell me. I deserve the unvarnished truth."

"Let's eat. Take a seat at the bar, and I'll make you a plate of rice and roll." He chuckled at his own joke.

Inside his mind, Bratten laughed out loud. *Oh, Alex, still trying to make jokes. Rice and roll.*

Alex blurted, "You never got my jokes."

Lauren's fork froze before reaching her mouth. "I've never heard your jokes."

"He's in my head. I feel like James McAvoy in *Split*, 'et cetera, et cetera.'"

Lauren laughed, "That was a good one, Alex." She took a bite of rice.

Oh, Alex, I miss you too.

Alex bit into the roll when the doorbell chimed. He took another bite and drank a few gulps of water. "Be right back. That's Logan."

Lauren ate a few bites of sushi when Alex returned with Logan.

Logan appeared to be in his late forties, maybe early fifties. He stood three or four inches taller than Alex and weighed perhaps two hundred and fifty pounds. Solid white hair with deep brown eyes, sun-weathered face, and skin.

Alex brought Logan into the kitchen. "Lauren, this is Logan. Logan, this is Lauren."

Logan nodded. "Nice to meetcha." He carried an old battered brown leather briefcase. "You two go ahead and finish eating. I'll sit at the table and pull out my files."

Alex said, "We have plenty. Want a plate?"

Logan smacked his belly. "Healthy food would send my stomach into shock." He chuckled.

Lauren glanced at Alex. "I'm full." She joined Logan at the table as Alex wolfed down the rest of his meal.

"May I call you Logan?" she said.

"Sure thing. Everybody else does." He laid several manila folders onto the black rectangle table. "I'm going to cut to the chase. I've concentrated most of my efforts on Mason. Before moving to Las Vegas, he served in the Middle East, where the authorities arrested him for a Ponzi scheme, but the authorities didn't have enough evidence to pursue a trial, and he was released. Many of his files from the Middle East are classified."

Logan handed Lauren a photo of Mason in uniform. "I've interviewed most of his first unit and just started tracking down the second one. I've also done an initial background check on Drake Properties employees and started on the subs, contractors, and sales reps. From the intel I've gathered, Mason worked for a private military company in counter-narcotics and counterterrorism. Some of his unit members have disappeared without a trace."

Lauren said, "Oh my god."

"Oh, Mason worked on military orders, but sometimes orders get blurred, and lines get crossed. You don't mess around with a man like Mason. He led covert operations in the dead of night. There's no telling how many people died. Relentless killings that some of the members of his unit dropped their baskets. You know..."

Logan held his hands up, palms out. "Well, most of those who know Mason won't talk. Not yet, anyway. Pretty sure he's not working alone. Very tight-lipped friends. Mrs. Drake, Alex, not that I mind the work, but you may need to consider letting the authorities handle the case. The feds are involved now. Lauren, someone killed your husband and burned your house down last night. You're in way over your head."

Lauren went over to her bag and handed him the anonymous card inside the ziplock baggie. "I've received two cards. Detective Stone has one of them."

Logan reached into his briefcase and brought out a small container of vinyl gloves. He lifted the card and read the sentence. "Hm. I'll send it to the lab."

Alex said, "We also have a storage device belonging to Bratten, which may have all the evidence we need to arrest

Mason. We made you a copy and made several others for safekeeping."

Logan tented his fingers. "Mason knows powerful people. Monies changed hands enough times to make Mason look legit. Everything with Drake Properties seems to be on the up-and-up, but something about him stinks. I'm still digging. I won't stop."

Lauren's voice rose, "I have reason to believe that Mason was cooking the books at Drake Properties, and I'm certain some of the workers are illegals, and Bratten didn't stop him. He trusted Mason to arrange green cards. The books, the illegals, and Bratten wanting to get out of the partnership got him killed."

Logan raised a brow while twiddling his thumbs on the table. "Well, if what you're saying is true, you're in more danger than you realize. Does Drake Properties have an accounting firm?"

Alex leaned back in the black leather kitchen chair. "Of course, Langley and Associates."

Logan made a few notes on a yellow legal pad. "Alex, contact the insurance company and have them run a workmen's comp audit and request any claims in the last two years. Who handled the books at Drake Properties?"

Lauren said, "We have an accounting department at the office that works with the firm. But Rose Rossi may be involved too. I've called a staff meeting on Monday."

"Don't overplay your hand. Taxes brought down Capone," said Logan.

Lauren leaned in closer to Logan. "Bratten was trying to do the right thing. He wanted out. He told me the night he was killed. That's why he wanted to move to Wycliffe."

"Two wrongs don't make a right." Logan patted Lauren's hand. "Honey, you ain't the first person that's found out their spouse don't walk on water. My grannie used to tell me it was the small cracks in the dam that led to trouble downstream. Be careful working at Drake Properties. Let Mason think you're on board and not dissolving the business. Have you ever acted, Lauren?"

Lauren replied, "Yes. In high school."Logan sighed. "I hope you remember how to do it. You need to convince everyone at Drake Properties that business will continue. Any illegal activity, you call me. I have a friend on the force that moonlights on the side for me. The ECP could be compromised. Baby steps, but we'll nail them. I haven't lost a case yet. Don't intend to start now."

On an impulse, she hugged Logan's neck.

Alex went over and shook Logan's hand. "Can't thank you enough, my friend."

Chapter 6

After meeting with Lauren and Alex, Special Agent Logan Clarkson met with his team in the rented space next to the Drake Properties building. The bureau had sent some fresh recruits. He was getting up to speed on the case. Six Special Agents sat around a semicircle table. Two agents had worked with Logan in Vegas. All six worked undercover trying to crack the case, infiltrating the police department, Drake Properties, and city government.

Logan walked to the whiteboard with a chart of Mason's activities drawn out in a diagram stopping with Bratten Drake's death, followed by the explosion last night.

He said, "I've been following the actions of Mason Williams since before he left the Middle East. That's when his actions came to the bureau's attention. He signed on with a private military unit, Southern Security. He met most of his connections during his tour, and from the information leaked, Mason and his band of brothers are trading illegal arms, smuggling contraband, and possible human trafficking."

He paced about the room. "Mason has connections with big money people, he has power in town, and his savvy techs are thwarting our efforts in his arrest. Here's what we believe:

Mason buys and sells large quantities of arms and trades them to the Evening Cartel in Mexico and a few cartels in South America. He's created a homegrown terrorist cell that has no regard for the laws of the United States. He's our main suspect in Bratten Drake's death and the explosion last night. We get him, and we get the cell."

Clicking on the overhead projector, Logan started moving through surveillance photos. "Mason met Andre Rossi in Iraq, which led to him meeting Rose who worked for Drake Properties. I believe he purposely set up Bratten Drake and uses Drake Properties as a front to run arms and other illegal activity."

Special Agent Haddock said, "Why would he kill Mr. Drake if he used the business as a front?"

Logan pointed at the female agent. "Great question and I think I have the answer. Bratten wanted to dissolve the LLC. He wanted to move to Wycliffe. Bratten got in Mason's way. Proving it is another story. I'm using my cover as a private investigator to get close to the case. I've requested Special Agents Taniguchi Akio and Elys Angwin to help redirect the business server to gain access to Mason's computer."

Logan looked at each agent and said, "We use the board for any new information. I want to go old school with our paperwork. I don't want one of the brotherhood gaining access to our activities. Special Agent Woods is working on compiling updated information on the brotherhood. Any breakthroughs?"

Woods glanced at his notebook. "Preliminaries are sketchy at best. But, hypothetically, the new pilot, Dennis Kelton, is on a watch list."

Logan said, "What do the locals get from the home invasion? Any prints?"

Woods shook his head no.

"Make yourselves invisible, and we'll meet back here Monday night." Logan dismissed the team.

A fall storm front woke Lauren from a restless sleep. She grabbed her silk robe, cinching the sash at her waist, then tiptoed out of the bedroom down the stairs into the kitchen for something to drink. She dispensed water into a cup and took a sip when warm, strong hands slid around her waist, untying her robe.

Sucking in a breath, she didn't move when Bratten whispered, "Alex is asleep."

His body pressed against hers, surging desire waking her libido and making her tummy clench. Lauren's head lolled back against his shoulder while his hands slid between her silks. A breathy sigh escaped his mouth. "Be quiet. Don't make a sound."

Her heart beat wildly in her chest.

Lauren gazed into his eyes, but the dark kept her from seeing if his eyes were blue or green. "Don't. We shouldn't."

He crushed his lips against hers with an all-consuming passion, pressing his rock-hard pectorals against her thin robe. Goosebumps rolled over her skin. She gasped as his fingers explored her body over the soft material. His tongue trailed along her throat as his fingers slid down her sides and between her legs.

Raking her fingers through his hair, Lauren tugged his head back. "Bratten, stop."

He cupped her ass, pulling her next to him, grinding his hips into hers. "Oh, honey, he's sleeping."

She slid her hands down his chest. "I want you. I won't lie." She cupped his firm glutes. "These don't belong to you. They belong to Alex. Those lips I just kissed belong to Alex." Releasing her grip, Lauren intertwined her fingers, raising them to her lips and kissing his fingertips. "These are Alex's fingers. Shall I go on and tell you what else belongs to Alex? You may have temporarily taken over his consciousness, but Alex's physical body does not belong to you."

Bratten sighed, "Killjoy."

"We're treading in the uncharted territory linking your spirit to Alex's body. Listening to you and seeing Alex is confusing for me. I want to love you, but I will be making love to Alex. I'm not sure I can separate the two."

He turned his back to her, and she wrapped her arms around his waist. "How about you sleep with me? Sleep, mind you. We can hold each other, at least."

He turned and pressed his forehead to hers. "I know I'm using Alex. But with his body, I can touch you again. Kiss you again. How could I not want to make love to my wife just one more time?"

Lauren held his hand and pulled him into the living area. "Don't guilt me. The only way I'd make love to you again is with Alex's consent. I don't want to ask him. It's not fair for either of us to ask that of him. And, just say, for instance, I like making love to Alex. Where does that leave you?"

He released a long exhale. "Oh, god, I guess we need to think it through. Up until now, Alex's infatuation with you never bothered me, but if you fall in love with him, that's a whole different story. I don't want to think about it. Let's go to your room before we wake him up. I want to hold you."

Lauren held his hand as they ascended the stairs and went into the guest bedroom. She took off her robe and slid between the sheets.

He got into bed and drew her to his chest. "I always loved your sweet scent. Sunshine and flowers."

Lauren nudged against his neck. "You must promise to go to Alex's room before he wakes up."

He kissed the top of her head. "I promise. Oh, baby, I miss everything about you. I miss us."

Wrapping her arms around his waist, she pressed the side of her face to his bare chest. The beating of Alex's heart made her weep. "I miss you too."

Waking up alone on Saturday morning after the sweet reunion in the kitchen made Lauren hug her pillow and inhale. It was Alex's scent on the pillowcase, not Bratten's. Lauren had enough drama in her life without the added conflict of emotions over Bratten and Alex.

She reached over the bed and grabbed her laptop from the floor. She powered it on and then searched channeling, popping up many pages to different sites. Most people channeled spirits, not the other way around.

Alex knocked on the door and stepped into the room. Smiling, he said, "I brought you a cup of coffee, two creams, two sugars."

Aw, Alex remembered how she liked her coffee. "Thank you."

"That is how you like it?" His eyes roamed her silk nightie. She swallowed hard. "Um, you might want to cover up."

"Oh, I'm sorry. Would you hand me my robe?"

Alex picked up the robe and held it in his hands for a few minutes. "I dreamed I kissed you last night. That I..." His lashes lowered then he locked eyes with hers. His breathing became rapid as he handed her the robe. "Do you have something you want to tell me?"

"Sit down, Alex."

"No. I think I'll stand." Alex crossed his arms over his chest.

"Bratten sort of took over your body last night." She threw her palm out. "Nothing happened." Lauren relayed the talk she had with Bratten omitting the steamy kitchen encounter. "I'd never take advantage of you, Alex. I respect your friendship too much." She moved over to the edge of the bed and looked up into his eyes.

"I thought I was dreaming. Bratten's gotta realize that because he can take over my consciousness, I can still remember most of what he's saying and doing." He extended his hands outward. "I have feelings for you, Lauren. Kissing you only intensifies them." Alex raked his fingers through his hair and walked out of the room.

Lauren jumped off the bed and reached for his forearm. "Alex."

He searched her eyes, and his gaze lowered to her mouth. He leaned in softly, sliding his hand to the back of her neck, and kissed her so tenderly she'd thought her heart would break. "I love you. All of you, and I'll do anything for you. All you have to do is ask."

Lauren pulled back and held onto his arms. "Alex, I wouldn't use you like that, ever." Their relationship seemed to shift. Her awareness of him, the intense way he looked at her, his energy of love radiating into her soul. She wrestled with the burgeoning feelings for Alex, then reached up on tiptoe and kissed his cheek.

The palm of his hand caressed her face. "Fair enough. I'm going for a run. Want to come with?"

"I would, but I don't have running shoes or workout clothes. While you're out, I think I'll surf the net and order some things. What are your plans for the day?" She leaned against the wall's cool surface.

"Whatever you want, sweetheart." He smiled, and she watched him leave the room.

Her heart skipped a beat, thinking of a future that may never come to fruition.

Monday morning, Lauren pretended everything was routine at work. The only change in Drake Properties was her assistant. She moved Rose into acquisitions and hired a new personal assistant, Jennifer Hayden. Angeline had recommended her.

She walked into the conference room with the department heads. All turned and fell silent as she made her way to the head of the table. She didn't sit. "I appreciate everyone coming today. Where's Mason?"

The on-site supervisor shifted in his seat and said, "He had another meeting he couldn't cancel but said you could go on without him. I'm sure he'll catch up later."

Lauren straightened her shoulders and lifted her chin. "I am staying on as CEO of Drake Properties. I own the company's controlling interest and want to ensure each of you the business will continue with a few changes."

She looked at the accounting manager, Agnes Snell. "Expect a workman's comp audit from our insurance carrier. I've also hired an independent firm to audit the business books to comply with any rules or regulations with the city, state, and federal offices." The room stilled.

She took a breath, walked over to the back table, and poured a cup of coffee. She looked up as Mason entered the conference room.

Lauren said, "I want to bring Drake Properties into the twenty-first century by installing an online vendor portal for better workflow, scheduling subs, estimating project costs and sales as well as components allowing visualization of the design during each phase of a project. The software company is setting up mandatory training sessions. I'll email out the schedule dates and times later."

Mason coughed loudly and said, "Lauren, I've manually controlled the job site scheduling for the last two years. I've personally supervised each project while Bratten developed the customers."

She nodded and smiled. "I know. You'll agree that our checks and balances will streamline our process and save the company time and money. You and I will discuss it privately after the meeting if you wish." Reading over past project files, it was hard for Lauren to determine what was real and what was a fabrication. "But overall, the business runs smoothly, largely due to the employees in this room."

Lauren walked back to the table and sat down. "Questions?"

Most of the employees looked at Mason. It took an enormous amount of composure not to scream.

Mason stood and addressed the group. "People, Lauren is doing what she thinks is best for the company. I intend to work with her to make sure her transition into Bratten's shoes is as effortless as possible." He looked at her and winked.

Lauren forced a smile. "Thank you, Mason. Are there any other questions?" No one made a response. "My door is always open. Have a good day."

Juan García waited until the room emptied, then approached Lauren. "I have questions about the migrant workers."

She noticed that Mason lingered outside the conference room. "Juan? Is that correct?"

"My name is Juan. Mr. Mason promised green cards and the chance to become naturalized citizens."

"I will do what is in my power to help you. Your English is perfect. It's one of the requirements to become a citizen. I checked over the weekend, and the Center for Learning offers classes every Tuesday night. I'll pay for any worker who wishes to take the classes and any paperwork to expedite the process. Alex Charland is my attorney. He works with several local charities, which may help too. Get me a list and address of those interested, Juan, and I'll inquire about the next steps."

He nodded and grinned. "Thank you, Mrs. Drake." He left the room.

Lauren intended to help Bratten right some of his wrongs. She gathered her notes and coffee cup and stepped into the hallway. Mason walked with her to her office. She could practically see steam escaping his ears.

She went to her desk as Mason closed the door. Opening the laptop, Lauren looked up and asked, "What's up?"

Mason paced around the room and stopped next to the land plat of Wycliffe Avenue. "I know you don't trust me, but your husband did." He turned to face Lauren. "We should've discussed the online vendor portal. I've been scheduling the job site operations for the last two years."

She leaned back in her chair. "The new software will increase our profits. I thought you'd be pleased that I'm not dissolving the business or taking you to court. Can't we work together, Mason?" She said with a honeyed sweetness that made her sick. Logan said, act. *Ugh.*

Mason's eyes raked over her body. "I'd like nothing more than to work with you. I'm here for you, day or night." He went to her desk, reached for her hand, and squeezed it.

Lauren fought the urge to yank her hand away and instead slowly withdrew it. "Good. I'm glad we've come to a meeting of the minds." *Slimy bastard.* She leaned her forearms on the desk.

Mason turned to leave, but he stopped. "Did you know that Bratten and Alex fought before he died? Right here in this very office."

"What do you mean they fought? What kind of fight?"

"It's not common knowledge. May I sit down?"

"Sure." She pressed her hands together, palms down on the desk.

"A few days before Bratten died, I walked in here around closing time and caught them arguing about Rose. Alex thought Bratten was having an affair and threatened to tell you about it. He shouted that Bratten wasn't good enough for you. Bratten laughed it off at first until he realized Alex was serious. Bratten slammed him against the wall and told him to stay away from you. From there, the shouting escalated into a punching match. I broke it up."

"Bratten and Alex have been best friends for years."

"Yeah, I get it. Don't you see how all this makes sense? And, now, you've moved in with Alex. He couldn't have calculated a better outcome, and you fell hook, line, and sinker."

Lauren trembled with anger but used her willpower to remain calm. Panic set in, making her armpits sweat. "My husband never cheated on me. Never. Whether Rose had feelings for Bratten is irrelevant. He isn't here to defend himself, is he? And if the shoe were on the other foot, and I was in Rose's position, I would've fallen for him too. Bratten Drake was the best man I've ever known."

"If you choose to ignore the signs, that's on you unless you and Alex planned his murder. Bratten's death would be a convenient way to inherit his fortune."

Gripping the edge of the desk, Lauren pushed away and stood. She had no intention of expressing her anger, frustration, and confusion with Mason. Lauren concentrated on breathing to calm her rage. Lauren said with all the control she could muster, "I have a call to make. Thanks for the info."

Mason said, "Lauren, if you would allow—"

She interrupted. "Please leave, Mason."

He opened the door and left.

Lauren's knees buckled.

Her assistant, Jennifer, rushed into the room as she slumped to the floor. "Mrs. Drake, are you all right?"

Lauren's voice cracked, "I'm okay. It's low blood sugar," she lied. She didn't want to unload on Jennifer, and she didn't wish to spread office gossip.

Jennifer helped Lauren to her feet. "Do you want a soda? Water or coffee?"

"I'll stop by the break room for a drink after going to the restroom." She shook her head slightly. "I have several drafts on my desk. Would you proof for me? I'll be back in a minute."

Jennifer nodded, and Lauren handed her the sheets.

Lauren headed down the hallway and entered the bath-room. She didn't care what other people thought about her. She didn't have anything to hide.

Locking the bathroom door, she moved over to the sink and turned on the water. She cupped her hands and splashed her face, then patted it dry with a paper towel. Leaving the facilities, she took a right instead of left, then overheard Rose. She pressed her back against the wall.

Rose said, "I don't like what you're doing to Lauren. Surely, there's another way."

Mason replied, "I know what I'm doing."

Lauren wanted to sprint away but remained in case Mason said something to incriminate himself.

"Look, Rosie, I'm doing the right thing here. Either you're on board, or you're not. I have a meeting in twenty minutes. Keep tabs on Lauren through Jennifer. Do what you must to friend the girl. It's the only way, I promise. Trust me?"

Rose replied, "Yes."

What were Mason and Rose planning to do to her?

Turning abruptly, Lauren went into the office supply room, shutting the door behind her. Her migraine returned with a vengeance throbbing her head with constant pounding, mak-ing even her hair hurt. She could deal with physical pain. Emotionally, not so much, but she'd buck up and do what needed to be done. She was determined to find out who killed Bratten before someone else died.

Lauren worked until after dark. She hadn't found anything in Rose's email. Lauren watched out her office window as the parking lot emptied. She waited another thirty minutes to make sure all employees were gone, and then she went to the offices to confirm. She walked into Rose's office and searched on Rose's desk and in her file cabinets for anything about Bratten that was personal. Nothing.

She slid into Rose's chair and tapped on the mouse. Rose's computer screen lit, requiring a login. Lauren entered Rose's login from Drake Properties, which she found through their site email info. The user info was correct, but the password was wrong.

Lauren tried several combinations of passwords to no avail. Her face fell into her hands with a sense of defeat. She glanced up and looked at the photo of Rose's son as an infant, which had his birthdate, height, and weight. Lauren entered 041095197. Bingo!

Her heart beat like crazy as she scanned folders and files. Lauren entered Andre Rossi's name. Several unnamed folders popped up, so she took the USB out of her purse and copied the folders, then quickly entered Bratten's name. Nothing.

Something made her type "Alan" in the computer search—Bratten's middle name. A photo folder popped up, and Lauren's stomach dipped. She opened the folder, and her heart squeezed. Dozens of photos with Rose and Bratten at bars and social functions, laughing and partying. Most of the dates in the folders were before Lauren met Bratten, but several folders were after they started dating.

Lauren shook with anger. The last folder dated a year ago, Christmas. Bratten held a dark-haired boy with blue eyes. She copied the folders, forced a computer shutdown, and stalked out of Rose's office.

Lauren's nails bit into the palms of her hands.

How could he?

Mason told the truth.

That child had blue eyes. Coincidence?

Lauren packed up her laptop and glanced at her phone. Alex texted several times. She was too mad to respond. Lauren didn't trust herself to be around Alex if Bratten suddenly took over his body. She turned off the lights and locked up the office.

Everything that happened since Bratten died, plus the photos, made her snap. She pushed the ignition button and flew out of the parking lot. A couple of streets over, Lauren passed The Dirty Rat and slammed on her brakes, skidding to a stop. Thankfully, no car was behind her.

Half of the Drake employees drank beer after work nearly every day at The Dirty Rat. She put her vehicle in park, then looked in her purse, retrieving her credit card and car fob, shoving both in her pant pocket. She applied red lipstick, brushed her hair, and looked in the mirror.

What are you doing, Lauren?

Half the people there were probably responsible for Bratten's death. She'd be damned if she'd let those people intimidate her. They needed to see she wasn't scared. With no fear for her safety, she went inside the pub. Straightening her back, she did a catwalk up to the bar.

A woman tending a bar looked up and dropped her cigarette on the floor. "Ma'am, I believe you may have made a wrong turn. This ain't no place for you."

"Whiskey with a beer chaser. I don't care what kind of liquor or beer. Just keep it coming." She handed the woman her credit card and glared.

"Your funeral." She walked to the cooler and pulled out a beer.

Lauren tilted her head and asked, "What did you say?"

"Nothing." The older woman popped the beer open. "We don't have cold mugs."

"Is there a reason you don't like me?" Lauren took a long pull from the beer.

"No, ma'am. We don't like cotton to be uppity around here." She poured Lauren a shot.

"What's your name?" Lauren picked up the shot and gulped. The whiskey burned going down her throat.

"Midge. That's what the regulars call me."

"I'm not uppity. I'm mad. I just found out my husband lied to me, and I can't do a thing to retaliate because he's dead. Another shot, please."

Midge's face relaxed, and she poured another shot. "Aw, you're the Drake widow?"

"That would be me." She sipped the whiskey and swiveled on the bar stool to look around the place. A group of men sat at the back table, two men played pool, and one man walked over to her.

"Mrs. Drake, what are you doing here?"

"Juan. How are you? Have a drink with the boss?" She guzzled the beer.

"You shouldn't be here, Mrs. Drake." Juan frowned and leaned against the bar top.

She looked over her shoulder and shouted, "How about I buy a round for the house?"

Several shouts of *all right, damn straight, and yeah* filtered through the place.

Midge shook her head and started stocking more beers in the cooler. "She's gonna be trouble, Juan."

Juan said, "*Si. Muchos* problems."

Lauren's phone buzzed. Alex called, and again she hit end call. She finished her beer and tapped the bottle on the bar. "One more, Midge. Hey, can I use my bar app for music in here?"

Juan said, "Yes, Mrs. Drake."

She placed her hand over Juan's and said, "I'm too young to be a ma'am or Mrs. Drake, while having a beer. Call me, Lauren."

A stout man with broad shoulders wearing a leather jacket and jeans walked inside the bar. He looked at Lauren and said, "Fuck me. What's she doing in here?"

Lauren narrowed her eyes and said, "What's it to you, Son of Anarchy?" She belted out a sharp-edged laugh.

The man went to the other side of Lauren. His eyes raked over her. "Uh, um. Does the boss know she's in here?" he asked Juan.

Juan shook his head. "No. You call him?"

"Hell naw. I ain't opening that can of worms. So, missy, what are *you* doing in *our* bar?"

Midge slid over a beer to Lauren. "She just got here, T-bone. She ain't staying long."

"Who says I'm not? I just bought a round for the house. I ordered music. I'm sick and tired of being sick and tired." Lauren took a drink of beer, then started peeling the paper off the bottle.

Lady Antebellum's "You Look Good" played through the speaker system. "Who wants to dance?" No one approached her. No one. "Fine. I'll dance by myself."

Lauren sashayed into an open area while raising her arms, slowly rotating her hips to the groove. She closed her eyes, not wanting to see the eyes of the onlookers. She danced for herself, releasing her pain and allowing the sexy tune to make love to her soul. Lauren glided across the beer-soaked floor in three-inch Louboutin's while her heart rate accelerated.

She tuned out the whistles and catcalls. The men didn't matter. Her body moved gracefully with her feet to the sultry beat. Hot blood coursed through her veins, drowning out the images of her husband with another woman. She was rotating slowly round and round, dancing her sorrow away as the song neared the end. With every pop of her hip, every flip of her hair, and dip of her knees, Lauren felt free.

Alex arrived home just before sunset. Lauren's car wasn't in the garage, and his stomach dipped. He'd texted and called her numerous times. He drove straight to Drake Properties.

He worried about her staff meeting. Had something happened to her?

He sped along the backstreets searching for Lauren's car at nearby shops, and she was nowhere in sight. "Lauren." He sighed.

Drake Properties parking lot was empty, so Alex kept driving the streets. He reached for his phone to call Logan, his guts twisting inside, afraid someone may have hurt Lauren.

Alex had almost given up when he passed The Dirty Rat and saw her vehicle. He pulled into the lot, parked, and sprinted through the front door. He stood speechless, watching her dance in front of half a dozen drunks. A whoosh of fury raged at the thoughts running through their inebriated brains.

Lauren's eyes were shut tight as she danced seductively. As the song neared, he saw tears trailing down her cheeks. *Oh, Lauren, you're breaking my heart.*

She stopped dancing and stood still for a long second, then opened her half-lidded eyes. She wet her lips. "Take me home, Alex."

The men roared and clapped, and he glared at them. "Shut the hell up." He turned to her and asked. "Where's your purse?"

"In my car. I've been drinking. Can't drive." She draped her arm around his waist and leaned against his chest. Lauren was crying.

He went to the bartender. "Cash her out."

"Done. Here's her card." Midge handed him Lauren's credit card.

A leather-clad man chuckled at the bar. "Hey, dude, need any help?"

"Leave them alone, T-bone," said Midge.

Alex glared at T-bone. "Back the fuck off." He helped Lauren out of the bar and into his SUV.

"Woman, do you know what you've put me through this afternoon? I've been looking for you for hours."

Her head fell back. "I'm mad. Alex, don't let Bratten take over, 'kay?"

"What happened, Lauren?"

"Bratten's a liar and a cheat. I have proof."

He buckled her up, then himself, before pulling onto the street for home. "I don't believe it. Whatever it is, there's an explanation."

"Still taking up for him?" She leaned her head on the passenger door window and sighed. "Alex, why did you come looking for me?"

His voice quivered. "Because I thought you were hurt. I thought they'd gotten to you too. Lauren, don't do that to me again." He trembled from head to toe with anger and frustration, fear and hatred toward those in the bar responsible for the devastation wreaked on his friend. Proof? He didn't have any. "Those men who watched you dance more than likely know what happened to Bratten, Angeline, and your home. What in God's name were you thinking?"

Reaching over the console, Lauren took his hand, bringing his fingertips to her lips. His heart melted with the emotion conveyed in her glimmering amber-colored eyes visible in the dimly lit vehicle.

"I'm sorry." She pressed kisses on the back of his hand. "I didn't mean to upset or frighten you." She held his hand in hers. "I saw red, Alex. I wasn't thinking. I have images of Bratten with Rose. I wanted to get back at him. I didn't care what happened to me. I don't care what those assholes in the bar think. I want them to know that I'm not scared, even though I am."

He exhaled, withdrawing his hand from Lauren's, and gripped the steering wheel. "Pretty sure word will spread, and you'll face employees tomorrow."

"I drank and danced. I didn't strip down naked."

After securing the SUV in the garage, he got out and didn't look back at her. Her foolish act in the bar could've gotten her killed. He didn't think he could take much more drama.

Lauren caught up in the kitchen, wrapped her arms around his neck, and pulled him to her. "Make love to me, please, Alex."

He withdrew and stepped back against the countertop. "I will not make love to you while you're drunk. I don't want a one-night or be your rebound man. Don't you get it? I want something more than sex." He arched a brow and smirked. "Don't get me wrong, I'm a fan of sex, but I need more in my life. I want something to build on, and as much as I want you, I won't blow a chance at the real thing."

Tilting her head, she said, "I fell hard and fast for Bratten. His love burned brightly, often leaving me breathless. I understand you want more. I'm not ready to give you more. I'm not sure I'll ever be ready." Her hands moved over her body, her gaze lifted to his with wanton desire. "This is what I have to offer. My body, not my heart, not my soul. If you don't want it, then I won't offer it to you again." Her lashes lowered, and she bit her bottom lip.

The flames ignited a whirlwind of emotions as he cursed his traitorous body. Lauren turned to walk away, and he reached for her, spinning her around, scooping her into his arms, covering her mouth with his lips.

Lauren's hands ran up his back, her fingernails digging into his shirt.

Her delicious body wrapped itself around his, the curve of her hips grinding into his hips. His hands moved from her slight waist up to her perfectly shaped breasts. The scent of her arousal was Alex's undoing as he laid her back on the kitchen table, cranking up an insatiable need to be inside her. His wildest fantasies were running rampant in his mind.

Lauren moaned, "Oh, Alex," pulling him back to her mouth. Her tongue danced with his, enticing him further.

Roaring entered his brain with such force that it knocked him away from Lauren. He held the sides of his head as the roaring continued.

Lauren screamed, "What's wrong? What's happening?"

"You son of a bitch," Bratten screamed in Alex's mind. "You're my best friend. She's my wife." The wild guttural cry echoed again, sending Alex crashing to the floor.

Lauren ran to him and placed her arms around him, and Alex shouted, "No. Bratten's in my head."

The anger in her voice rose, and she twisted Alex's face to meet hers. "Leave him alone, cheater." Lauren grabbed her purse from the barstool, searched, and pulled out her phone, bringing images to the screen. "See, you bastard." She slid photos across the screen until the roaring stopped in Alex's head.

Alex scooted against the kitchen wall with his arms wrapped around his knees, drawn to his chest. "Thanks. He was screaming like a madman. I guess I don't blame him. I can't make love to you. I know Bratten's technically dead, but he's very much alive in my brain. Geesh, that hurt."

She slid over next to him and leaned her head against his shoulder. "I'm sorry, Alex. It's my fault."

"Let me see those photos again." Alex reached for her phone and pulled up the images. Every image except Bratten with Rose's son was innocent. "I was the one who took those photos. Bratten wasn't cheating on you. That photo with Rose's son doesn't prove the boy is his child. If you want to leave no room for doubt, then have a DNA test run. The hospital still has Bratten's files, and I could submit a formal request."

She looked at him with tears in her eyes. "Really? He didn't cheat?"

Slowly, Alex shook his head. "I don't think so. My heart is breaking, babe. I love him, but I'm in love with you. It's late. We both have to work tomorrow. Let's give whatever happened tonight a few days to sink in before talking about it."

She reached over and kissed his forehead. "I have feelings for you too. I'm confused, exhausted, overwhelmed, and I don't want to hurt you. Please don't beat yourself up. I wanted you as much as you wanted me. That's the truth."

Alex stayed on the floor, watching Lauren retreat up the stairs. He didn't move until she closed her bedroom door. "Bratten?"

Bratten didn't reply.

"I won't apologize for my feelings, but I am sorry for acting on them."

Alex made a vow. "I'll keep my distance from her, romantically speaking. But, if Lauren's feelings for me change, she and I deserve a chance. Do you agree?"

Bratten replied with a whisper, "Yes."

Alex went upstairs, took off his clothes, and fell into bed.

He'd allowed Lauren to take over his rational mind.

He stayed in control over countless situations, prosecuted thousands of cases, and dated more beautiful women than most men did in a lifetime. But Lauren had seeped into the marrow of his bones. Her angelic face, sweet voice, and the heady scent of her ebony hair permeated his brain.

Even though, and maybe despite the havoc in her life, he loved her. Her spirit, grit, tears, and sorrow had turned him into a lovesick teenager. He was thinking of her and wanting her to be *the one.*

Mine.

That's what he wanted. That's what he dreamed.

Chapter 7

Mason sat in his recliner, sipping beer, eating chips, and watching the football game. His phone buzzed a few times before he picked it up. "What is it?" he shouted.

"Mason, it's Midge. You better get down to the bar. T-bone is beating the shit out of Juan."

He shook his head. "Why? What started it?"

"Hm. That Drake woman came to the bar tonight. Got the boys all riled up, and when she left, well, you know how T-bone makes crude comments about women. Juan had a thing for the widow and threw the first punch. The next thing I knew, T-bone pummeled him. T-bone is batshit crazy."

"I'll be there in ten minutes. Get one of the other boys to take Juan out back." He slid out of the chair, pulling on his jeans and boots. He grabbed a hoodie off the back-door rack and stalked into the garage.

Less than ten minutes later, Mason pulled around to the back of The Dirty Rat. Juan lay on the ground, almost unrecognizable. He opened the back passenger door to his SUV. "Damn it to hell." He went to the young man. "Juan, son, can you hear me?"

Juan slowly nodded.

Mason picked him up and put him in the vehicle. "I'm taking you to the ER. Man, Juan, T-bone is a wild man. Not worth fighting over a woman, even if she is your boss."

Juan groaned but didn't speak.

"Look, boy, I'll take care of the hospital. Don't tell them anything. I'll see you're taken care of, and your family will still get cash." He glanced over the back seat. Juan didn't move. "Juan?"

"Shit." Juan was unconscious. He accelerated speed onto the interstate to catch the new exit to the hospital. A few minutes later, Mason parked next to the ER wing. He stopped the truck and pulled Juan out, then carried him into the hospital.

One of the nurses at the check-in desk rushed to help him. She placed Juan in a wheelchair and ran him through the double doors into the ER.

The check-in nurse behind the counter said, "You'll need to fill out forms for the patient." She handed him a clipboard.

Mason said, "He works for me. Will he be all right?"

"What happened?"

Mason replied, "He got in a fight. A friend of his called me."

The nurse tapped away on her keyboard. "He's in a patient room if you'd like to go back and wait."

Mason nodded and followed her into an empty patient room. "Where is he?"

"X-rays and then CT. It's going to be a while. You don't meet caring people like you often. Mr.?" The nurse keyed in notes into her smart tablet.

"Mr. Mason Williams. I own Drake Properties."

The nurse said, "I remember Mr. Drake."

"Good man. If Juan needs an emergency contact, here's my card." He handed the nurse his info.

She didn't accept the card. "Someone from accounts payable will be in soon to pick up the forms." She hugged the tablet next to her chest.

"I'll be responsible for payment." Mason took a seat next to the counter and leaned back in the chair.

"Tell accounts payable." The nurse left the room.

He filled out the form to the best of his ability when a young man with accounts payable came in. Mason handed him the paperwork, and the man looked them over. He asked a few questions that Mason refused to answer.

"I will be responsible for payment. Here's my credit card."

"I'll make a copy and return in a bit with his hospital packet. If Mr. Garcia stays overnight, you'll receive a passcode. There's a toll-free number you can call if you have questions. Thank you."

Mason watched the hospital rep leave and nodded off to sleep while Juan went through a battery of tests.

Finally, Juan was rolled back into the room on a hospital bed, followed by a gorgeous doctor, Michelle Evans. "Mr. Williams, Juan has lacerations and bruises to eighty percent of his body. Juan has four broken ribs and his left wrist fracture. We want to keep him overnight to keep an eye on the trauma to his brain. I notified the local authorities. The next twenty-four hours are critical."

Damn it to hell. Mason nodded to the doctor, then pulled his phone from his jean pocket and texted the Colonel.

Mason: T-bone put Juan in the hospital. The ER doc notified the authorities.

Several minutes passed before he received a reply.

Colonel: Animals. I can't get through one day without one of you animals doing something stupid. I'll put a call into the station and make sure one of ours intercepts.

Mason wondered why Lauren came to the pub.

Did she have a death wish?

He called Mole. "Were you there tonight?"

Mole replied, "Yeah, man, the widow put on a show until Charland dragged her out. T-bone got so jacked that Juan punched him. It was ugly. I finally pulled T-bone off the boy, or he'd be dead. Is he dead?"

"No. Not yet. You need to access the hospital's system, make Juan's balance zero, remove my name from any records, and scramble the video surveillance. Got it?" He strode down the hospital corridor and out the door. It wasn't the first time the RB hacked into the hospital server.

"Sure thing, boss."

Mason ended the call. He'd pick up the kid tomorrow and take him to the farm to recuperate and arrange for one of Juan's amigos, Diego, to stay with him. The farm's fridge stayed stocked, the pantry had staples, and he'd only leave an untraceable phone for emergency use.

The farm needed winterizing anyway. Mason would leave Diego a list of chores.

It could take Juan weeks to recover if he made it. Juan had become an essential part of his team, and T-bone just fucked it up. Juan's interpretation skills and loyalty to the RB were valuable commodities not often found.

T-bone would reimburse the RB for the expenses incurred or find himself at the bottom of the Cumberland River.

Two years ago, the move to Tennessee had been the right one. He just had to bide his time until the insurance money came in and then escape across the border to the RB villa with his family.

He drove home in silence.

Mason threw his keys in the bowl on the table next to the door.

Rose came to him and circled her arms around his neck. "Is everything okay?"

"No, darling." He withdrew her arms and held her hand. "Is the boy asleep?"

"Yes. Sound asleep."

Mason pulled Rose into their bedroom and closed the door. He reached into his chest's top drawer, pulled out a cat of nine tails, and handed it to Rose. Mason dropped to his knees and ripped off his hoodie and T-shirt. "I need blood for my sins."

Rose locked the door. She knew what he needed even if she didn't understand it. With every lash, she recited a verse from The Lord's Prayer. Sins mounted daily, and eventually, the angel of death would catch up with him.

Ray answered his mobile. "Hey, Pete, I have you on speaker."

Pete replied, "No problem. You told me to let you know if anything came in the station regarding Mason or his boys. Well, we just got a call from the hospital. Mason brought in a badly beaten illegal to the ER. The young man is staying overnight. Want me to check into it?"

"Nah, I just left the diner. I'll stop by the hospital. Wonder who the boy is?"

"No clue. Okay, if you're sure, I'm leaving the station. It's been a long day."

"It's been a long year." Ray ended the call and made his way to the hospital. He went to the check-in desk and flashed his badge. "I need to speak with the doctor on call about a patient brought in earlier."

The nurse said, "Please have a seat, and I'll page Dr. Evans."

Ray leaned against the counter. "I'll need access to patient records too."

"You'll have to speak with accounts payable. They require a warrant to release paperwork regarding patient information."

He nodded.

Ray interviewed Dr. Evans first and gave her his card. From her description, Mason brought in Juan. The doctor suggested he come back tomorrow to see the patient. Juan was on morphine for the pain, so Ray went to the business office.

The silence in the hospital late at night gave him the creeps as death lurked in the shadows waiting for another soul.

The hospital accounts payable person became irate when he pulled up Juan's records for Ray. Apparently, tampering had occurred. She wouldn't expound except to tell him that Juan's account was paid in full.

Ray wasn't surprised.

The next day at the office was awkward, but Lauren ignored the whispers and the stares. She thought for sure Mason would've mentioned her unbridled promenade in the pub, but no one said anything, so she swept it.

Over the next couple of days, Alex didn't return home until after Lauren went to bed at night and left before she woke in the mornings. He was ignoring her. So, she didn't press him. Honestly, she wasn't ready to talk about her plea for sex.

He'd communicated by text that Logan's IT team confirmed Friday night's sting at Drake Properties.

Thursday after work, Lauren checked Alex's mailbox. *Another card.* A storm brewed in the October sky, so she waited until she got inside the house to open it. She placed the mail along with the card on the island bar and went to the wine cooler, pulling out a bottle of merlot.

After pouring a glass, she sat at the bar. Her fingers ran across the top of the envelope, and she hesitated to open it.

Alex came in the back door. He stopped, staring at the envelope in her hand. "Another one?"

She nodded. "I hate opening it. Every time I feel like I'm crawling out of the funk, something else happens to drag me back down. Every crime violates my sanity, choking the life out of me."

"Do you want me to open it?"

"Do you mind?" she asked.

Alex placed his briefcase on the side table and looked under the sink for a pair of latex gloves he used for cooking. He opened the kitchen desk drawer and retrieved a letter opener.

Lauren handed him the card, and he slid the blade's tip, breaking the seal.

The card read: *Be careful what you ask for— you just might get it.*

Alex called Logan and relayed the context of the note. He went outside onto the patio and shut the door.

Lauren banged on the glass door, and Alex shook his head with a frown. She threw her palms out and mouthed, *what the hell?*

A few minutes later, Alex came inside, went into the kitchen, and put the card in a plastic baggie.

"Alex, what were you talking about? Tell me."

Alex grabbed the bottle of wine and poured a glass. He took a sip and then placed the stemware on the island counter. "A couple of days ago, Juan was found nearly beaten to death outside The Dirty Rat. From the nurse's description, the man who brought Juan into the ER was Mason. Logan said Juan defended your honor after you left Monday night."

She gasped as her hand flew to her mouth. "Oh, no. Poor Juan. How is he? And Mason took him to the ER?"

"No record of it. Someone tampered with the hospital footage, and Juan's patient records have disappeared. Sounds familiar, huh?" His gaze met hers. "Juan checked out of the hospital. No one knows his whereabouts."

She plopped onto the bar stool. "It's my fault. I-I don't know what to do. What does Logan say?"

"Logan is looking for him. He has contacts with the ECP and the Feds. If they find Juan, and if he turns state evidence against Mason, they can place him in protective custody."

"He's not a citizen. He won't talk. I must do something. I can't sit by and do nothing."

Alex sat on the stool next to her. "Unfortunately, there's nothing you can do. The authorities are looking for Juan. Logan and I believe the anonymous card is about your dance in the pub and the injured Juan."

Her fingers went into fists. "Stupid, stupid thing I did. I wasn't thinking straight. I haven't been thinking right since Bratten died. It's always one thing after another. Will it ever stop??"

Alex placed his hand on her knee. "Not until they charge someone for the crimes against Bratten and your family, and now, Juan. Someone in authority and with some pull is helping Mason."

"That makes sense. Weeks have flown by, and the authorities are no closer to an arrest than the day of Bratten's murder. I'm going to bed. All I want to do is sleep. I'm overwhelmed and weighted down. Alex, I'm sorry for the pub, for making an ass out of myself. If I hadn't stopped and started drinking, Juan wouldn't have been hurt."

Alex reached for her hand, and she withdrew it.

"I can't talk anymore."

Bratten hovered in the corner of the room, watching Lauren on bended knees, her head bowed, and she prayed, "Please God, show me the way. I'm lost. I don't know what to do. Help me, please. Open my eyes that I might see, open my ears that I may hear, and know your direction in my life. Protect my family, Alex, and my workers. Protect them from harm. I'll gladly lay down my life for theirs."

Bratten pressed a kiss to the top of her head and watched her crawl into bed. For most of the night, Lauren tossed and turned in her sleep.

He whispered in her ear, "If I could go back in time, I'd make different choices, so we could live until we're old and wrinkly. If I could do it over again, my love, I would've never hired Rose. I would've never met Mason. I'd still have a pulse, and I'd be sleeping with you in our bed instead of watching you cry yourself to sleep."

Friday night at eight o'clock, Lauren met Logan, and the IT asset, Elys Angwin, at Harold's Grocery, one street behind Drake Properties. At Logan's suggestion, she drove to the front of her building and parked if anyone saw the lights.

Alex and the other IT asset, Taniguchi Akio, worked from Alex's home office to set up the remote server.

Logan entered the back entrance of Drake Properties and did a sweep for bugs, then called Lauren to bring in Elys. If all goes well, they should have the entire system copied to the remote server in less than an hour.

Operation Judgment Day began with thick tension in the air.

Elys entered the internal server room and logged into the mainframe undetected. "Cloud computing and virtualization technologies add significant complexity to the network." She keyed feverishly, and without looking at Lauren, she added, "Someone's added a URL Blacklist. Tricky. Someone's already redirected the server to a different remote server. I'll replicate and link into both before redirecting, so the ghost user won't know that we've hacked their system. Don't send any private emails from your office."

Lauren paced the floor while Elys worked and talked data system jargon that wasn't a part of her vocabulary. She hadn't used her work email a few times and nothing significant, but Bratten had used it daily.

Lauren jumped when her phone rang. "Logan?"

He said, "We have company."

"Oh, god. What do we do?" Lauren started wringing her hands, and sweat poured down her back.

"I'll handle it. How much time is left?"

Lauren looked at Elys. "Someone's here. Logan wants to know how much time?"

"Tell Logan not to sweat it. I'm almost done." Elys worked as if she had all night and the next day to finish.

Lauren envisioned Mason all commando bursting through the doors, guns blazing. She shook from head to toe in fear.

Elys got on her phone. "Akio, are we good on your end?" Elys nodded and smiled, then packed her gear. "Backdoor?"

Lauren said, "Yes. Ah, thanks."

"Don't mention it."

Lauren called Logan. "Elys has left the building."

Logan said, "Hey, doll, you ready for dinner?"

"Logan? Are you still talking to someone?"

"Yes."

"Do I come out?"

"Uh, huh."

"Okay, I'm on the way."

Lauren released a long sigh and then turned off the lights in her office and the data room. She flipped on the little desk lamp at the receptionist's desk before entering the security code to lock up.

Outside Logan talked to Rose.

Lauren tilted her head and frowned. "Rose, what are you doing here?"

"I left some paperwork I wanted to work on over the weekend," Rose replied super sweetly.

Lauren zipped up her coat and said, "No, need Rose. Everyone deserves some time off." She wasn't going to explain to Logan or introduce him because she had no idea what he had told Rose. Lauren reached up on tiptoe and kissed Logan's cheek. "I'm starving. Let's get out of here. And Rose, you go home and enjoy your weekend." She shooed Rose away.

Rose raised her chin and turned, and walked to her car with a quick nod.

Logan got into the passenger seat of Lauren's car while she slid behind the steering wheel.

Logan said, "She's gone. Breathe, Lauren."

"What did you tell Rose?"

"I said I was an old friend of Bratten's and was taking you out on the town."

"She bought it?"

Logan squeezed her hand. "Yeah, pretty sure she bought it."

Lauren nodded. "Good. Let's go to Alex's."

He said, "First, let's swing by The Dirty Rat. I have a hunch."

"But Mason is there." She started the car, backed out of the parking spot, and then pulled onto the side street.

"That's right. I want to see if Rose went to the pub too."

"You think Rose is with Mason?"

"I do." Logan seemed angry, so she stayed quiet.

Lauren drove a couple of blocks from the office and slowly pulled into the pub's full parking lot. She spotted Mason's Tundra and then saw Rose's Acura. "You are good."

His face relaxed. Chuckling, he said, "That's why I get the big bucks."

"Do you know something you're not telling me? Who killed Bratten?"

"Lauren, I know Mason and his friends are bad people. If I were you, I wouldn't step foot inside Drake Properties until the investigation is over. And stay out of The Dirty Rat. Do I know beyond a reasonable doubt who killed your husband? No."

"I don't have a choice. I'm not quitting Drake Properties. I know I'm in danger, but who will if I don't fight for Bratten?"

Back at Alex's home office, Lauren talked a mile a minute about the operation and the encounter with Rose. Logan filled Alex in on the details she left out, then he and Akio said their goodbyes.

"So, Rose and Mason are a thing?" Alex sipped on a bottle of water.

Lauren replied, "Yes. I think so. Do you want to start searching the files?"

"Not tonight, Nancy Drew. It's time for a break. Besides, I owe you an apology for shutting you out this week. Monday night..."

She pressed her fingers to his lips. "Don't. You don't owe me anything. Any word of Juan?"

"No. It's hard to track someone that doesn't want to be found."

"Do you think that's it, or is he running from whoever beat him?"

"Both. If I were in Juan's shoes, I'd lay low too. But Logan promised to keep us updated." He reached up and pulled on his neck.

She walked around the back of his desk, and he raised a brow. "I give good neck rubs. Tilt your head down and relax." She ran her thumbs down the column of his neck, and a moan escaped his mouth. "Alex, your neck is filled with knots."

She pressed on one spot working the knot until it released. "You need to schedule with my massage therapist. One hour a week is worth a million bucks."

He turned around in the chair and grabbed her hands. Taking a breath, Alex said, "You were brave tonight. The files will be waiting for us in the morning. Why don't you relax, take a hot bath or read the book on your nightstand?"

She placed the palm of her hand on the curve of his strong jawline. "You're a good friend. I don't know what I'd do without you." She kissed the corner of his mouth softly, then stepped back and retreated from the room.

Part of her wanted to stay with Alex and see if he wanted to watch TV or a movie. Maybe have a cocktail and talk about anything other than problems. She stopped midway down the stairway and ran back up to the third floor into his office.

Alex looked up and grinned. "What'd you forget?"

"Let's go to dinner tomorrow night and maybe even dance at a club."

He chuckled. "Haven't you done enough dancing? Plus, I'm not as swift on my feet as Bratten."

"Ha, ha. It's fall, and downtown is decorated for Halloween. I need a bit of fun, something other than stressing twenty-four seven. What do you say? My treat."

"Well, since it's your treat, how can I refuse?"

She smiled. "Good. It's a date. Or, well, you know what I mean. Good night, Alex."

"Goodnight, Gidget."

In the corner of Alex's office, Bratten hovered. He watched the growing attraction between Lauren and Alex. He wanted Lauren's happiness, he wanted Alex's too, but damn it, Afterlife hurt.

Nancy and Aunt Lynda appeared beside him.

Nancy leaned against Bratten's arm. "Don't you think you should give them a chance? It won't develop into anything if it's not meant to be. Let them have tomorrow night without interference.

He turned to them. "I know you're right, but I want Lauren with me, not him."

Aunt Lynda placed her arm around his waist. "Life is short on Earth. She'll be with you again, someday."

Bratten frowned. "Yeah? What about Alex?"

Nancy smiled. "He will too."

Bratten threw his palms up in exasperation. "How does that work?"

Aunt Lynda chuckled. "It just does."

Chapter 8

Mason went to an emergency meeting of the RB called on Saturday morning. He walked into the back room of The Dirty Rat with two dozen homemade cinnamon rolls made by Rose. T-Bone, Mole, and Noxzema sat at the table drinking coffee and shooting the shit. "So, Mole, what's going on?"

"Gotta wait for the Colonel." Mole tore into a cinnamon roll. Mumbling with his mouth full, "Tell Rose, thanks. She's a damn good cook."

"I know." He rubbed his stomach. "My six-pack is turning into a twelve."

Guffaws erupted among the men.

The Colonel entered the room with a smile.

Mason said, "Did you get laid last night or what?"

The Colonel said, "I did. What's the emergency? It better be good because I left a sweet ass woman in my bed that I'd like to get back to." He grabbed a cup of coffee and a roll.

Mole gulped the rest of his coffee. "The feds hacked into the Drake Properties server last night." He threw up a hand and said, "I have it under control but thought everyone needed to chill on anything with the Net. If they're in the system, they're on our mobiles." He opened a box and dumped disposable phones on the table. "Grab the phone with your name on it."

The Colonel looked at Mason. His smile turned upside down. "Where are we on the insurance money?"

Mason leaned against the back bar. "The policy is still under investigation. The rep said that's the protocol for ten million."

"We can't afford to draw more attention to ourselves, T-bone." The Colonel glared at T-bone, then looked at each of them. "It's time to start redirecting our assets to a new location. It's time to move, my brothers. So, until we get the green light that the insurance money is transferred into our offshore account, whether it takes six days or six months, I expect you to act like choir boys. Let's concentrate on tying up loose ends, so when the time comes, we can get the hell out of this Podunk town with our brotherhood intact."

Mole chuckled. "Choirboys. That's us all right."

"Exemplary actions are required to get through this fiasco unscathed, and that's no laughing matter." The Colonel reached over and grabbed the phone with his name on it. "Now, if that's all, gentlemen, I have more pressing matters waiting for me at home."

He smacked Mason on the back, and Mason groaned and dipped away.

"Mason, man, are you still doing that shit?" The Colonel shook his head, and Mason didn't reply.

Operation Judgment Day was a great success, in Lauren's opinion. Saturday morning, she woke to an empty house. So, she worked on her laptop and ordered a portable hotspot for Drake Properties, then hit some clothing stores to replace essentials lost in the fire.

After brewing the perfect cup of coffee, Lauren strolled on the patio to enjoy the unseasonably warm weather. The sun rose over the treetops, and she exhaled. Alex's backyard was very Zen. She watched the busy squirrels gather stores for the upcoming winter.

A bible verse came to her mind.

To everything, there is a season and a time to every purpose under the heaven: A time to be born, and a time to pluck up what is planted; a time to kill, and a time to heal; a time to break down, and a time to build up; a time to weep and a time to laugh; a time to mourn, and a time to dance.

Lauren couldn't remember the rest, but the verse in Ecclesiastes spoke to her soul. She'd been too ensconced in grief to recognize the joy in her life. Her parents, Angeline and her family, and Alex filled her heart with great joy, and she didn't tell them enough.

She picked up her mobile and called Angeline, but it went straight to voicemail. "Hey, sister. I didn't want much. I just wanted to tell you I love you, and I'm glad you're in my life." She ended the call and left a similar message on her parents' phone.

Alex opened the glass door and stepped onto the patio. "It's nice out here."

"Join me." She grinned.

His face lit with a smile. "Alrighty." He stretched out onto the chaise lounge, throwing his right arm over his head.

She looked at Alex. Tomorrow held no guarantee. On impulse, she pushed him over and snuggled next to him. He draped an arm around her as she watched the white clouds lazily float in the deep blue sky.

"It's been a while since we enjoyed a relaxing Saturday morning."

She tilted her head to Alex's face, and blue eyes stared back at her. She didn't say anything. She draped her arm around him.

Bratten rubbed her back. "So, you and Alex are going on a date?"

Lauren shifted to get a better look at him. "It's not a date. I need a night without thinking, a relaxing dinner and maybe some dancing. Do you mind? Alex has been good to me. He's had a lot of pressure placed on him that he didn't ask for."

Bratten looked up at the sky. "But you like Alex. I mean really like him."

She hesitated, then said, "Yes. I like Alex. It doesn't stop me from loving you because I care for him."

"Lauren, I won't move on until I know you're safe, but if me appearing from time to time upsets you, I'll stop."

"I'm not ready to let you go. Although, I think there should be some separation. Don't get me wrong, but I wanted to lie next to Alex, nothing more like today. Just the closeness of him makes me breathe a little easier. Please don't misunderstand. I love you, but you popping into Alex's body throws me into an emotional tailspin. I see the big picture. You passed away, and even though your spirit is here, your physical body is gone. There's no going back, no do-overs, only moving forward. Do you understand what I'm trying to say?"

"I'm interrupting your grieving process. I get it. I don't want you to be lonely. I want you to love life. I've learned how to move about this realm without a body. So, I don't have to use Alex as a vessel anymore. Would seeing my spirit upset you? I watch you sleep sometimes. Does that creep you out?"

She rose to a sitting position and placed her hand on his chest. "No. I love that you're watching over me. I'm..."

"Torn?"

"There you go again, finishing my sentences." She chuckled. "Yes. I'm torn. I will never love anyone as I love you."

"Yeah?"

"Yeah."

He took her hand and kissed it. "You deserve a new beginning, a new chance at life without me. My mom said I needed to give you and Alex space. She said, if you were meant to be, you would be. If not, what's the harm, right?"

"That's one way of looking at it."

"Lauren, I'll give you space. If you need me, call my name, and I'll be there." Bratten's eyes faded into Alex's green ones.

Alex squeezed her hand. "So, he's not going to use me as a vessel?"

"That's what he said."

"Hey, I have an idea. Let's get ready and drive to Nashville. We'll grab something to eat and stroll Broadway, then maybe if you're lucky, we'll dance." He winked.

She threw her head back and laughed. "Give me an hour."

Alex showered and shaved, then dressed in jeans, a black turtleneck, and a blazer. He changed at least six times before exiting the main bedroom. He went downstairs and found Lauren waiting on the off-white sofa. She wore dark denim with a cream-colored tunic and a long gray sweater paired with short black boots.

"It's a gorgeous afternoon. I'm excited." She jumped from the couch and slung the strap of her black purse with fringe over her shoulder.

"Do you want to take the Jeep or my SUV?" he asked.

"SUV. We can park downtown and walk. I just checked. No rain in the forecast."

"Let's go."

Nashville was a destination town for tourists. It had an eclectic vibe of music, fashion, and food. In August, Alex had traveled with Bratten to watch a preseason football game in one of his vendor suites. After the game, they hit the downtown bars and spent the night at the Omni.

Lauren listened to music on Spotify on the drive to Nashville, singing loudly to her favorite tunes. He wanted her to have a good time. They were friends, and maybe she'd see him as something other than a crutch after some time.

"I booked dinner reservations at Bob's. Incredible steaks and chops. After dinner, I thought we'd park there and make our way to Broad." He rested his hand on the console between them.

"I haven't been to Nashville since last spring. Smart Media had a conference at the Sheraton. We rode on a party bus one night." She laughed. "It's funny what people do with a few drinks in them. A bachelorette party was on board, and oh my, those girls were wild."

He glanced at her and grinned. "You mean to tell me you weren't wild on yours?"

She blushed. "I didn't have a large wedding, remember? Although, Angeline and I did spend the day at a spa. So, what did you and Bratten do?"

Alex's brows popped. "I'll never tell." He laughed, and she goosed him in the ribs. "Honest to God, we went to Wycliffe. There's an old college bar where we used to hang out. We drank beer and talked about the glory days. No strippers, I swear. I'd never seen him so happy as the day he married you."

"I wasn't going to talk about him today. But you and I will always be connected with Bratten for the rest of our lives, so there's no way to pussyfoot around it. Let's make a pact that nothing is off-limits regarding Bratten. That way, neither of us will feel awkward talking about him. He said that if you and I were meant to be, it would happen, and if not, we're sweating the small stuff."

"Agreed."

Forty minutes later, Alex veered off the ramp toward Second Avenue and used valet parking at the Omni. He ushered Lauren inside a sports bar for a cocktail. "We have a few minutes before our reservation. Let's check the football scores in the South."

"Did you play football?"

He leaned against the bar counter. "Nah, I had to study hard to get into law school. I didn't have much time for extracurriculars. Did you play sports?"

She hopped on the stool and said, "Not on a team, but I love to play golf. Do you play?"

"Love it. The hardest game I've ever played. Wanna play a round sometime?"

"I'd love to."

Alex couldn't remember a more fun dinner. He and Lauren laughed and talked while sampling each other's food.

Lauren told him stories about her and Angeline growing up. She went to college, and Angeline married Eron. "We're sisters and best friends. She's a mother hen, but I love the fuss most of the time. Since my parents retired, they travel a lot, so Angeline's been my anchor, especially since Bratten died.

"I get it. It's nice to have people in our lives we can have fun with and still depend on."

Alex paid their tab, and they exited the door onto the noisy Nashville streets.

Lower Broad stood in the shadow of the famous Ryman Auditorium. Quickly, Alex and Lauren were elbowed deep with tourists. Honky Tonks lined both sides of the streets.

They held hands strolling on the sidewalk, drifting into different bars to catch a country tune and a beer, then moved on to the next one. Time whizzed by, and he and Lauren were on an alcoholic high. He didn't want to think about tomorrow's hangover.

Alex was hyped up and loved the laughter and good times. Lauren moved smoothly through the crowds like parting the Red Sea. The loud music and people buzzed his brain as he got into the rhythm of the night.

Alex leaned in and shouted over the noise, "If I'm driving, I need to stop drinking."

Lauren pulled him along the street. "Oh, no, not yet. We're having too much fun, and I have points on my card. Let's stay at the hotel. I'll check my app." Lauren pulled out her phone, tapping a few times. "There, I booked a double at the Omni. Let's check out this cute shop. I want to get a T-shirt."

"Okay, you win." He allowed her to drag him into the store full of country western attire with plenty of spangles, cowboy boots, hats, jeans, and shot glasses.

Lauren bought an *I love Nashville* T-shirt and another one that said, *Hey, Y'all.*

They ended up at a rooftop bar and grabbed two seats. The flickering glow of the Nashville lights, the moon, and the sublime music with Lauren at his side filled his soul with joy. It was magical.

A few people danced on the floor while others chatted with friends.

Alex ordered a couple of beers.

With a raised brow, Lauren asked, "Think you've had enough liquid courage to dance with me?"

He pushed away from the stool and gave her a bow. He said, "I'd be obliged, ma'am, with his best Southern drawl."

They stepped onto the dance floor, and the band's lead singer belted out a slow, sad song. Alex drew Lauren to him, and she nudged into the hollow part of his throat. Her arms circled his neck. The heady mixture of vanilla and lavender engulfed his senses. Her breasts crushed into his chest, making his heart pound.

He trembled as she gazed into his eyes with shyness, and he smiled. She returned a brilliant grin radiating her beauty both inside and out.

They moved effortlessly with the music. Alex leaned in, kissing Lauren gently and with sweet tenderness. Her fingers trailed down his back, and her kisses seared his lips with agonizing perfection. The song ended, leaving him breathless.

Lauren reached up on tiptoe, and she kissed his cheek. "Oh, Alex, I love tonight."

He brushed his cheek next to hers. "The best night ever." Alex knew he'd never love another like her standing in the middle of the dance floor.

Nearing midnight, Alex and Lauren strolled back to the hotel. He said, "We can Uber if you don't want to spend the night."

"I want to spend the night." She followed Alex to the check-in, and he tried to pay, but she insisted and gave the desk clerk her card. "Reservation for Lauren Drake."

The desk counter attendant keyed in her information and said, "Ah, I'm sorry, but no doubles are available. I do have one king. Busy weekend with festivals and football games."

Lauren looked at Alex and said, "Do you mind?"

He shook his head. Maybe they had a couch, or he could sleep on the floor.

The attendant said, "Luggage?"

"No."

A slow smile spread across the attendant's lips. "Well, go to the elevators to the third floor. You'll see the room numbers. Enjoy."

Lauren rolled her eyes and walked away from the counter toward the elevators. "His mind's in the gutter. Look, Alex, no pressure here. We're just sleeping, right?"

Alex replied, "Of course. No pressure. It's better than getting a DUI."

"I'm going to be straight with you, Alex. I love kissing you, but I'm not ready to move beyond, but it's a step toward something I believe is special. I want to be completely honest. I'm afraid of much more."

He held her hand and squeezed. "And you think I'm not? My feelings for you scare the hell out of me. Slow is good, but I warn you, I snore, especially after drinking fifty beers."

She threw her head back and laughed. "I know you snore."

"Ouch. Is it that bad?"

"Nah."

Alex said, "Okay, to strip to my boxers?"

She snickered. "Alex, I've seen you in boxers. I'm wearing my new T-shirt." She went into the bathroom and closed the door.

He stripped down, laid his clothes on the chair, and went to the corner window. The room had an excellent view of downtown. He stepped over to the desk and flipped through the room service menu. "Hey, what do you want from room service?"

"Cheeseburger, fries and a coke, extra ketchup and mustard. Hm. Also, chocolate pie."

He called in a double order and groaned. "I'll have to run five extra miles from all the calories next week."

Lauren pushed her head under his left arm, then hooked her right arm around his waist. She giggled, staring at the skyline, "But it sure was fun."

They ate and talked until the wee hours of the morning and fell asleep in each other's arms in the king-size bed.

Over the next several weeks, Lauren and Alex grew closer. He'd given her the space she needed both at home and work, plus the added benefit of no one trying to kill her lately.

Detective Stone and Logan Clarkson worked leads on Bratten's death while she and Alex sifted through years of data from the Drake Properties server, trying to link Mason or Rose to Bratten's death.

Over time, Lauren experienced some stages of grief and the first milestones without Bratten's physical presence, like her birthday on Halloween. He used to go all out on Halloween with crazy decorations, costumes, and extravagant parties.

But this year, Lauren spent the night with Angeline, Eron, and the twins, and Alex joined her family at their church's annual Harvest Hoedown with game booths, bouncing playhouses, and rock climbing walls.

Wycliffe Avenue broke ground on the first of November. With Eron as the main contractor, Lauren developed hands-on experience with the project. She worked hard, and one evening, she realized she'd worked the whole day without thinking of Bratten once.

Lauren closed the office the day before Thanksgiving and walked to her car. Her stomach clenched when she found a bullet hole with a note on her windshield. *Time's almost up.*

She called Logan and Detective Stone. Alex had gone on an overnight business trip, and she didn't want to alarm anyone.

Her life had run too smoothly of late.

She'd prayed the terror was over.

It wasn't.

The authorities took her vehicle, and Logan gave her a ride home. He said, "I want to place a guard on you."

"Whatever you think, Logan, but no one saw anything. Honestly, I think the person is trying to intimidate me. If they wanted me dead, I'd be six feet under."

"Honestly? I think we have more than one perpetrator. I'm not trying to scare you, but I believe we have a group of individuals working together. The notes almost seemed like a warning, and I think there may be an internal struggle within the group. I agree. If they wanted you dead, you wouldn't be here."

"I've done some real soul searching and lots of praying. I've come to terms with death. I'm at peace if I go today, tomorrow, or thirty years from now. It's strange how people don't communicate feelings about death more. Death is a part of life, and none of us are getting out of here alive."

Lauren and Alex went to Angeline's to celebrate the Thanksgiving holiday with her mom and dad. The crisp November air cut to the bone as they stepped up to the front entrance.

Angeline met them at the door with hugs and kisses. Inside the house, the fireplace crackled with flames. Angeline had already decorated for Christmas. There's nothing like holiday traditions and decorations to warm up feelings of love, nostalgia, and memories.

Alex threw up his hand with a wave. "Hey, everyone." Then he stepped into the kitchen. "Eron, you need any help carving the turkey?"

Lauren went over to the island to help Angeline and Carol make the final preparations for the feast while her dad and the kids watched the Thanksgiving parades on television with squeals and peals of laughter.

Carol stepped over and hugged Alex. "It's been too long, dear. How are you?"

"I'm good. How are you and Dan?"

Dan replied over his shoulder, "Never better. Need any help?"

Carol waved both hands. "No, honey. You enjoy the kids."

Angeline talked about their recent fall trip to the beach. Her hands moved a mile a minute while she spoke. "We rented a beachfront house with four bedrooms. We had great weather, and the kids had so much fun boogie boarding. Eron and I spent every second together with long walks on the beach, and one night we took the kids crabbing." She sighed. "I'm ready to go back."

Lauren sipped a glass of red wine, watching Alex. He seemed at home with her family.

Over dinner, they shared lots of laughter and talked about everything from politics to football, but no one mentioned Bratten. It was the first Thanksgiving without him since he and Lauren were married.

It was weird.

Bratten had been an enormous part of her family life, and no one wanted to discuss his death or even talk about him. As if he never existed, or they feared that talking about Bratten would place a damper on the festive mood.

It made Lauren angry and sad, but she just missed Bratten most of all.

After dinner, Lauren helped Angeline clear away the dishes while everyone else went into the living area to watch football.

Inside the kitchen, Angeline asked, "So, how are you and Alex getting along?"

"Um, good, I guess." She filled the dishwasher, then turned it on.

Angeline wiped down the countertops. "I think you like Alex more than you care to admit. He seems to be crazy about you. Would it hurt to at least give Alex a chance?"

"I'm not ready for that kind of relationship." She threw the dishtowel on the counter. "And you haven't asked me how I feel about Bratten not being here today or on my birthday. That hurts. I care for Alex, but Bratten is still alive in my heart. Alex is a good friend, but I'm afraid that's all he'll ever be."

Alex stood in the doorway with his mouth gaped. His pained expression was a punch to her gut. With a ragged breath, he said, "Well, I guess I should've stayed in the den watching the second quarter. Um, Angeline, could you give Lauren a ride home?"

Lauren said, "Oh, Alex. I didn't mean anything by it. I can come with you. We're almost finished with dishes."

"I'll wait in the car. Tell your family it was good to see them." With two long strides, he was out the back door.

Lauren placed her hand on her forehead. "Oh, good grief. What do I do now?"

Angeline folded the dishtowel and placed it on the hook. "Alex is in love with you, Lauren. I didn't mention Bratten because I didn't want to upset you. I miss Bratten too. But he wouldn't want you wallowing around in sorrow. What does your heart tell you to do?"

"I can't go there. I can't. I thought Alex and I had an understanding. We were getting along fine as roommates."

Eron walked into the kitchen. "Hey, what happened to everyone?"

She said, "I've made a mess of things with Alex. I gotta go. Let me kiss Mom and Dad goodbye. Sorry, hate to eat and run, you guys."

Angeline kissed her cheeks. "Talk to Alex. Tell him how you feel. He deserves nothing less than the truth."

"I'll try. Thanks for cooking, sister. Love you."

Lauren slipped into the car, and Alex didn't look at her. The deafening silence grated on her nerves during the drive home.

Alex parked in the garage and slammed the door after getting out. She followed him inside and watched him race upstairs, appearing minutes later in his running gear. He paused at the door; his jaw ticked as if he wanted to say something, but he didn't.

Lauren watched him run down the drive onto the street. She waited for his return on the front porch. She buttoned up her coat tight, slipped on her gloves, and pulled on her winter hat.

The sun faded into night, and the lights of the neighboring house came on one by one. White chimney smoke filtered in the air from directly across the street. The laughter from children playing outside echoed and diminished.

Lauren shivered from the cold and finally gave up and went inside. For a while, she paced back and forth in front of the fireplace, then took the stairs to the guest room. She jumped in the shower, towel-dried off, put on her pajamas, and pulled on warm socks.

Lauren picked up her book on the nightstand and jumped into bed, flipping to the marked page. She read the same passage at least a dozen times. She'd hurt Alex by sending him mixed messages, but she was twisted inside.

Finally, the front door opened and closed softly. Footfalls ascended the staircase. Lauren straightened her back as she heard Alex approach her room. She listened to his labored breaths, but he didn't come in.

Butterflies danced in her stomach. "Alex?"

"Yeah?"

"Would you come in for a minute?" Lauren slung her legs over to the bed and placed her hands on her lap.

Sweating from head to toe, Alex stepped into the room. "You don't have to say anything. I don't want to hear it anyway."

Her cheeks burned under his smoldering stare. "You don't want to hear what?"

Closing his eyes and with pain in his voice, he added, "How much you still love Bratten, and how we'll always be friends." His jaw clenched tight.

"I'll never stop loving Bratten. He's a part of me, and yes, I hope we are friends. Good friends. You're also part of my life." She slipped out of bed and walked over to him.

Alex glanced at the floor as she reached over and tipped his chin upward. "Are we still friends?"

Tingles shot up her spine as he cupped her face. His touch sent zinging awareness to all her body parts that had been dormant. He searched her eyes, nose, and mouth with blatant lust, weakening her knees on shaky legs. His look burned with passion.

She held her breath. The air constricted in her lungs. The awkward silence stretched as Alex's gaze roamed her body. He lowered his head, his lips so close that she parted her lips in anticipation.

Waiting.

Was Alex going to kiss her?

She bit her bottom lip when he didn't and glanced at her feet. She trembled with desire.

Her gaze lifted, and in an instant, Alex pressed her against the wall, his mouth covering hers in a hot, intense kiss with rough desperation buzzing her brain with extraordinary energy blasting her core with fluttering.

He inhaled and nipped her neck, then pulled back slightly, staring at her with a look melting the ice around her cold heart. His hands slid to her face, thumbs caressing the hollow curve in her cheekbones as she reached up, twisting her fingers in his sweat-drenched hair.

Her mind reeled.

Her heart pounded.

Was he going to kiss her again or make her beg?

She didn't speak, and neither did he. Everything seemed to fade from existence except for him and her and those spectacular green eyes.

Reality crashed in around her.

Alex's kiss made her feel both alive and crestfallen. He held her tight with strong arms.

She waited and wondered what would happen next?

Where did they go from here?

Two choices. *Love him or let him go.*

Alex made her laugh and dance. He gave her the will to keep living. He placed himself in harm's way to protect her time and again. Death and danger could rear its ugly head in a blink of an eye, destroying either them or both.

Lauren closed her eyes and swayed against him. She blinked several times as he lowered his lips to hers, much gentler than before, but his kiss grew bolder as a moan escaped his mouth. He drew her closer, his fingers fisted into her hair. Her fingernails dug into the flesh of his back as the last vestige of her restraint released.

"I want all of you if you don't want the same. If all we'll ever be is friends, then this will be our last kiss."

Time suspended.

The weight of his gaze drowned her in raw emotions.

Tears welled in her eyes. "I know what it feels like to fall in love. I know what it feels like to lose love. I'm-I'm afraid. If I lose you, I'll lose myself forever. I'm just starting to heal. Do you understand?"

"You won't lose me."

"You can't promise me that because the one certain thing in life— is death comes for us all."

Alex brushed his fingertips along the curve of her cheek. "Honey, I can't promise I won't die before you do, but I can promise to be there for you with every step life offers. Give me the word, Lauren Drake, and I'll wait a lifetime for you. I've waited this long what's a little longer?"

Lauren cupped his face and smiled. "Word." He frowned, and she kissed him.

"I want you too. Give me some more time, please. I want you, Alex. Truly I do."

He held her hands and took a step back. "I'll place the sun, moon, and stars at your feet if that's what it takes. Stay with me tonight? Let me hold you."

Lauren twisted her wedding ring around and around her finger.

Alex's eyes blinked, turning blue.

She took a deep breath and lifted her chin. "I-I don't know what you want me to say. I didn't expect it. I certainly didn't plan it."

Bratten's eyes glowed with the shimmer of the ocean on a sunny day. "I don't blame you for wanting to feel alive when you are alive. Alex is here, and I'm haunting you."

He paced the room with his hands extended. "I said I wouldn't use him again, but damn it, I'm mad, and I'm jealous. All I want is your happiness. All I want is your safety. But damn it, I want you too. *I want you!* I want to be alive." He cried and pulled her to the bed. She leaned against his chest.

Looking into Bratten's eyes, she whispered, "I love you. I will always love you."

He leaned down and kissed the tip of her nose. "I know you love me, honey. I know I must let you go. I will always love you too. Remember, love is limitless, and it has no boundaries, babe. Love for each of us is immeasurable but also different. I don't blame you or Alex. If I could pick anyone for you in my place, it'd be him."

"How can I love Alex and still love you?"

He nudged her cheek. "Baby, the more you love, the more limitless love becomes. You will always have me. Here." He placed his hand over her heart. "And here." He kissed her head. "You'll always love me, but it's okay to love Alex too."

Chapter 9

After the holidays, a winter blast hit the town during the first week of January. Lauren worked on her laptop from home. She'd given her employees the day off. The temperatures plummeted to single digits with wind chill below zero.

The logs in Alex's fireplace warmed the room. All the Christmas decorations were removed, but the evergreen scent lingered.

She sipped on hot chocolate when Bratten materialized like an apparition. She said, "I see you, Bratten Drake."

"I've learned a few more tricks from the other side. Where's Alex?"

"He went to the store for food and stuff. Why?"

"I know who is sending you the cards."

Lauren stiffened. "Who?"

"Rose."

"Why is she trying to scare me?" She closed her laptop and tucked her feet under her legs.

"I don't think she's trying to scare you. If you dig deeper into Rose's files, you'll understand why she's trying to warn you."

Bewildered, Lauren said, "She hates me. Why would she want to warn me?"

He hovered next to her. "I met Andre on the other side."

Lauren's hand flew to her mouth. "You're kidding me?"

"Serious as a heart attack."

"Not funny, Bratten. So, what happened?"

"In her filing cabinet at the office, search for a folder named *assassino amichevole*. It's Italian for the *friendly killer*. It contains a letter from Andre and the official letter from Southern Security. Andre was killed by someone he thought was his friend."

She frowned and shrugged. "Who? Mason?"

"Andre didn't see the killer. He was on a mission and among friends. He was shot in the back."

She propped her elbow on the sofa. "Mason. It must be him. If it is, then why is Rose living with him?"

"Not a hundred percent sure. Maybe Rose is frightened for her son. Go through her file cabinets at the office. I'm telling you, it's the smoking freaking gun."

Lauren left Alex a note and took the Jeep to the office. Not a track had been made from the freshly fallen snow in the parking lot. She entered the office and searched each room to ensure she was alone.

Rose's door was locked, so she used the master key to enter. She opened the tall black filing cabinet, sifted through each drawer's folder, and came up empty. Behind Rose's desk, she pulled out the credenza filing cabinet. Same process, same result. Nothing.

She sat in Rose's chair and pulled out each drawer in the desk, careful to keep everything as Rose left it. In the bottom drawer on the right, Lauren found the folder under a box of stationary. She didn't take time to read. She raced to the copier, placed the documents into the feeder, and pressed copy.

Lauren shoved her documents into her brief bag and raced back to Rose's office, returning the folder to its rightful place, then locked Rose's door and headed toward the reception area. Rounding the corner, she smacked Mason's chest.

Her knees locked. "You scared me to death."

Mason held her arms. His eyes narrowed. "What are you doing here?"

Her pulse racing, her heart banging, she replied, "Making sure the sinks were dripping so the pipes won't freeze."

She shoved him away. "I could ask you the same thing."

"I left my iPad. Thought I'd catch up on the vendor portal."

"You can do that from your laptop." Her mobile rang, and she said, "I've gotta get this. Will you lock up? I was heading out."

He smirked and shrugged. "Sure. Black ice out there. Be safe."

"You too." She dashed out the front entrance and jumped into the Jeep, not looking back. Shaking, she plugged her phone into Bluetooth. "Alex. Sorry, I had to get a folder at the office. I'm on my way home."

"Be careful. Wrecks are everywhere. Especially on hills and overpasses."

"See you in a bit." Lauren ended the call. "Whew, that was close," she said aloud. She cranked up the defrost and punched on Spotify. "Quick thinking on the pipes too." She chuckled nervously.

It was mayhem driving on the roads. Cars and trucks were sliding into ditches or running into each other. Lauren prayed. Once she parked, she went through the garage into the mud-room to take off her winter gear and boots.

Alex sat at the bar in the kitchen. "Thank god. I was getting ready to come looking for you."

She plopped her bag on the bar stool. "I couldn't talk on the phone." She withdrew the copied documents—her heart near exploding. "Bratten appeared in his spirit form while you were at the store. These documents were on Rose's desk. They're supposed to prove Andre was shot by someone he trusted." She flipped through several pages until she came across Andre's letter.

She read it aloud:

Rose, my darling,

Your news at Christmas made me the happiest man in the world. I'm writing to you snail mail because I fear my emails aren't safe. I've submitted my resignation letter to the organization. You and our unborn child make me want to be a better man. I never expressed the love I have for you.

I told Mason that I was leaving. He indicated they'd never let me go. I know too much. I've seen too much, but I must try. I want a new life for us. I intend to leave after the mission tomorrow. Rose, don't trust anyone until you see me. Stay safe. Go live with your parents until I get home, then we're leaving and going where no one can find us.

Love with all my heart, Andre.

"Holy shit," Alex sighed.

"Here's the letter to Rose from Southern Security." She read:

It is with a heavy heart that I must inform you Andre Rossi was shot and killed by friendly fire. While we strive to maintain the utmost excellence with our personnel, human mistakes and errors happen. When a death occurs during a mission, our organization takes accountability first, notifying the commanding officer, and then a notification is sent to the base. The investigation into Andre Rossi's death was ruled accidental. Our priority is to inform the next of kin promptly of the incident. However, in the field of operations, sometimes events take longer to report. Due to security reasons, some of the details have been omitted in the attached report.

Southern Security encloses a check from Andre Rossi's life insurance policy.

My deepest sympathies are with you during your time of grief.

Chaplain Adam Sloane

Lauren paled and handed the letter to Alex. "They killed him, just like they killed Bratten. How many have died?" she shouted and pounded her fist on the island counter.

"The photos in Rose's folder date before Andre Rossi's military service. They were in love, Alex. But a few years after working for Southern Security, Andre's images changed. Rose's smiles seemed fake. Then, Rose tells him they're having a child, and he has hope, and they kill him!"

Her fingers trembled holding Andre's letter. "He told Mason he was leaving. Then he gets shot in the back."

Alex ran his hands through his hair as he scanned the pages. "Look on the back page. Someone wrote 'Bullshit' in red letters: Colonel, T-bone, Mole, Noxzema, and Mason. Mason's name is circled." He handed the page to Lauren.

"Oh my god. Mason works for Drake Properties. I met T-bone at The Dirty Rat. But who are the others? How in the world did Rose end up with Mason?" Lauren asked.

"I'm not sure. But it indicates that more than one person is responsible for Bratten's death. Lauren, this may be a terrorist cell. I'm calling Logan." He punched Logan's number from his contacts on his phone. "Logan, I hate to ask, but can you come over? We have a situation."

Logan coughed loudly on the phone. "Alex, sorry, I dozed off. Give me a few minutes, and I'll head your way."

"Be careful, man. A major snowstorm's heading our way," said Alex.

Logan entered a group text to his team leaders. Once, he read over Lauren's confiscated documents from Drake Properties. **The noose is tightening. The cell is here. Priority is to identify the Colonel before raiding The Dirty Rat. The snowstorm will slow efforts. Be careful out there.**

"Great work, Lauren. I have a job for you if you're ever interested. I don't want to worry you, but my team needs to vet each person on the back of the page."

Lauren frowned. "You're not sharing with Detective Stone?"

"I will share the information with the authorities, but trust me, sometimes going through legal channels slows the process. Give my team a few days to research, and I'll touch base with you and Alex. There's been no movement since Juan's disappearance. My gut tells me the responsible parties are in the process of fleeing, which makes them more dangerous. That's why it's been so quiet on the home front. The snow will bring everything to a standstill."

"Are my employees in danger?" Lauren asked.

"Carry on business as usual. For the time being, that's the safest plan."

Logan and his team were closing in on the Revolutionist Brotherhood by hacking into their cyber-underworld while trying to keep civilian casualties to a minimum. Alex and Lauren were at risk, but revealing the extent of the RB's crimes would only place them in more danger. Lauren secured documents made each of the brothers' suspects in another murder, Andre Rossi's.

The RB used three separate servers for privacy and to communicate with buyers and sellers around the world. They'd located two of the servers, and it was old-fashioned investigative trickery that tracked the RB to Eagle Creek, and with any luck, they'd bust the cell by spring. Redirecting Drake Properties' server had located the third and only a matter of time until an arrest came to the unnamed users.

After Logan left, Alex paced the room. "I don't think Logan is taking your safety seriously enough. You need to think about working from home until we find out what Rose is trying to tell you."

"Sit down; you're making me nervous." Lauren reached into her purse, pulled out a medicine bottle, popped a pill in her mouth, and then sipped on a glass of water.

"What are you taking?" he asked.

"My nerves are frayed, I have a splitting headache, and my freaking heart is skipping beats. It's a prescription my doctor gave me after Bratten died."

"You know there are more natural ways to deal with stress. Meditation and exercise, therapy, to name a few." He stretched on the couch and laid his head on the pillow, kicking off his shoes.

She joined him on the sofa. "You do that. My way is quicker. Put your feet in my lap. I don't mind."

He shifted around and placed his head in her lap and his feet on the pillow. "How's that?"

"Better." Lauren brushed the hair away from Alex's forehead. "The snow is coming down outside. It's as if God knows we need a reprieve. Eron changed the subject to update the vendor portal on the Wycliffe Avenue project. So far, we're on budget and on time."

"I say let's enjoy the break. Do you want to watch a movie?"

"Oh, I like sitting in front of the fire on a cold wintry night. Tell me something about your childhood."

"I don't talk about my childhood much."

"You don't have to." She caressed his face with a smile that warmed several degrees.

"It's tragic. I had a little brother. We were best friends. We did everything together. I trusted him with my life. Our family had a boat on the lake—we spent our summers swimming and skiing, camping and fishing. I miss them."

He sat up and stared into the flames of the fire. "My dad loved weaving stories, so on the trip home after an outing. Dad told this grand tale about a boy that raised a wolf pup. My brother and I listened to his every word. The winding two-lane road was steep. A tractor-trailer clipped our boat, and he lost control. Our car flipped down a steep hill. That's all I remember."

Lauren placed her arms around him. "Alex, I had no idea. I'm sorry."

"I missed their funerals. I never got to say goodbye. Life is this great big wondrous thing that's intangible. I suppose without the bad, we'd never appreciate the beauty. My grandmother taught me to get past the grief by pointing out the changing of seasons. As a kid, you don't pay attention, but after losing so much, I did. I still do. I think that's why I love running. I love the seasons changing and know after every winter, there is a spring."

They went back to the sofa, and Lauren slid onto his lap, placing an arm around his neck. "I want to run with you. I want to see the changes of the seasons with you."

Lauren's simple gesture and compassion after speaking of his family grounded him. She might not realize it yet, but Lauren loved him. The warmth of her love and understanding spread through him deeper with more complexities than he'd expected.

"I'd love for you to run with me. We'll go and get gear when the weather breaks."

They held each other, staring at the flickering flames as the snowflakes blanketed the ground.

Just living in the moment.

Chapter 10

Lauren woke to the scent of bacon and eggs. Her stomach growled, but she went into the bathroom and took a quick shower, brushed her teeth, and combed the tangled mess of her hair. She pulled on a black cable sweater with gray yoga pants and thick aloe vera socks.

She ran down the steps through the living area with its massive windows. The outside world had turned into a winter wonderland, making everything seem abnormally quiet.

Alex hummed a song cooking breakfast. Lauren allowed her eyes to roam his body with his back to her. His T-shirt stretched taut across his broad shoulders, and her gaze lowered to his tapered waist, breaking her breathing rhythm.

She wet her lips unconsciously, appraising his glutes that could bounce rocks.

He turned, and a lock of his silky black hair fell forward, nearly covering his right eye as he brushed it away from his face. "Good morning."

"Something smells great and not very healthy." She giggled while pulling the bar stool out to sit on.

"What's the old saying? If you can't beat 'em, join 'em. I know you have an affinity for Applewood bacon, scrambled eggs, and Starbucks Pike Roast." Alex scraped the scrambled eggs onto the plate next to the bacon, then placed it in front of her.

"Somebody's good at buttering up." She took a bite of bacon and moaned in delight.

Alex punched the button on the Keurig, brewing her a cup of coffee. "Two sugars in the raw and two creams, right?"

"Yup." Lauren loved that Alex remembered her likes and dislikes.

He handed her a cup of coffee.

"Aren't you eating?" She sipped the delicious aromatic coffee. "Mmm."

"I got up early and ate oatmeal. What do you think about going sledding after breakfast?"

She nearly choked. "Sledding?"

He grinned as he brewed a cup of tea. "Yup. I have a sled in the garage. It's fun."

She chuckled. "I *know* it's fun. I haven't gone sledding in a decade."

"Good. You up for it?"

"I'm not sure if I have anything to wear for sledding." Lauren polished off the rest of her breakfast and wiped the corners of her mouth with a napkin.

Looking like a kid with his fingers in the cookie jar, Alex opened the pantry door and held up a black and pink ski suit with a matching winter hat, gloves, and boots. "The Superstore had them on sale."

"Aw, Alex. Thank you. Gimme a few minutes to dress." She kissed his cheek, then grabbed the apparel and accessories.

"I have to get dressed too. Race ya." He laughed.

"Hey, you wait for me." She raced him run up the stairs.

By the time she'd dressed, Alex had backed the Jeep out of the garage and laid on the horn. She ran out the side door along the sidewalk with her boots crunching in the snow, leaving deep tracks.

Inside the Jeep, she said, "Where are we going?"

"Have you ever gone four-wheeling in the snow?" He pulled out of the subdivision and took the back roads to the end of town.

"I can honestly say that I've never gone four-wheeling."

He yelled, "Yeah, baby—another first. I own a piece of property not far from here. I've been sitting on it to see if it goes commercial or stays residential. There's a great hill perfect for sledding."

Sunshine peeked through the clouds as Alex pulled down an isolated road off 231. He drove over the curb and up a moderate-size hill. Lauren was giddy as a kid again, jumping up and down as the Jeep stopped.

"Ready?"

"I'm ready."

Alex opened the back door to the Jeep and pulled out the wood toboggan. She joined him, looking at the snow-covered hill.

The brisk cold air made his cheeks rosy, and his green eyes sparkled like emeralds. "Once I'm on the sled, hop on my back."

She said, "Are you sure?"

He rolled his eyes. "Yeah, I'm sure."

Lauren and Alex whizzed down the hill into an open field free of trees and debris in minutes. She squealed with delight holding tightly to his shoulders. Alex maneuvered the sled to get maximum velocity carving out a path for future runs.

Lauren and Alex spent the next couple of hours having fun with gut-busting laughter. The whole day reminded her of childhood memories with Angeline in the snow. Lauren helped Alex build a giant snowman, and then she begged him to make angels in the snow.

Lauren and Alex looked up at the blue sky, lying in the snow. He reached for her gloved hand. "I love you."

Snow-covered, Lauren rolled onto her side, looking at Alex. "I'm falling in love with you too. I've been too afraid to say it out loud."

He grabbed her, rolling Lauren onto her back. Laughing, he shouted, "She loves me." Leaning in, he pressed feather-light kisses against her lips.

She passed the temptation phase and headlonged into feelings she hadn't wanted to admit.

He leaned in and said, "My heart is beating like crazy." He pressed his lips to hers.

Lauren grabbed his ski coat and yanked him closer, kissing him with fierceness. She melted into his embrace, tracing her tongue over his top lip, and he moaned.

Alex Charland loved her.

"Let's go home, Alex."

The light from the sun danced in his eyes, and his sweet breath mingled with hers in the cold. "I like the sound of that."

Alex's heart hammered against his ribs on the drive home. The sexual tension in the air hung thick. Lauren held his hand tightly, tracing her thumb back and forth against the back of his hand.

Lauren studied his face as if she were looking at him for the first time. He pulled into the garage and turned off the ignition. The air backed up in his lungs as she leaned over, cupping his face and kissing him in a way that unleashed the animal inside him.

Just inside the back door, Lauren pulled on his jacket as he unzipped hers. Frantically and feverishly, their wet clothes started dropping to the floor. Their eyes held, unable to break the hypnotic connection, as Alex scooped her into his arms, carrying her through the house, then taking the stairs two at a time.

The setting sun seemed to match the fire in his heart, spreading deep oranges and reds through the wall of windows across the bedroom.

Sweat beaded on his forehead and down his back. His arms trembled, fighting the urge to throw Lauren on the bed. Instead, he gently placed her on the top of the covers.

She shoved the pillows to the floor and began pulling at his thermals, and he reached over, pulling her sweater over her head, revealing her pale pink bra.

He unclasped her bra and swallowed hard. "Beautiful."

She stripped off her yoga pants along with pick matching panties.

Somewhat nervous, he stammered, "Are you sure?"

Lauren's voice deepened, "Yes. I'm sure. I'm so sure."

He kept reminding himself to breathe. His fiery goddess reached up and pulled him to her. She sucked on his top lip, then gingerly slid her tongue into his mouth.

His breathing accelerated. Every cell, every molecule in his body belonged to Lauren. He loved her to the depths of his singing soul.

Her creamy skin was as soft as the misting snow. Her cheeks flushed with the color of a peach rose as Alex traced the outline of her arms.

She didn't speak but kept her eyes on him while tunneling her fingers through his hair.

"You and me, together, we fit," Lauren whispered almost breathlessly, their faces almost touching. "We match up like pieces to a puzzle that I'm just figuring out. I'm sorry it took me so long. I'm not expressing my words right."

He nudged her neck and nibbled. "Your words are perfect. You're beautiful, so damn beautiful."

She drew her fingers down his chest and over his abs, making him laugh. She gave him a wisp of a smile. "So, you're ticklish?"

"Very much." He kissed the inside of her wrist.

She trailed her fingers over his abs again, making him quiver under her touch. She reached out and held him in her arms.

Her gaze dropped to his mouth. She lowered and brushed her soft lips next to his, kissing and tugging on his bottom lip. Breathlessly, she said, "I want you, Alex." Her fingers eagerly explored his bare chest with apparent urgency, and she gasped. "I'm drowning with need here, Alex."

Alex fixated on her mouth. He couldn't think of anything but Lauren. Touching her, holding her, and making love to her.

Mine.

His throat cinched as he whispered, "I love you so much it's hard to breathe." Alex traced her bottom lip with his fingertip with an urge to bite it. Instead, he slowly prolonged her anticipation, teasing and licking the seams of her mouth.

She panted, "Kiss me, please."

He leaned in, tugging, sucking her lip into his mouth but pulling back long enough to see the desire in her eyes for him.

Mine.

Alternating between bruising and gently brushing her lips with his, kissing her with ferocity, then flicking his tongue in and out and kissing again, he couldn't get enough of her and needed to please her.

He craved her.

Tingles raced up his spine as she traced her fingers along his shoulders and back. He propped on his elbow to marvel at her firm breasts, circling his thumb around the areola, pebbling her buds, and increasing her arousal and his own.

Lauren arched her back, and his eyes locked with hers as he took what she offered. Sweet and succulent. Alex savored the feel of her, overwhelming sensations flooding his body with a torrent of desire. His hands roamed and explored her hills and valleys. "Lauren, my sweet angel."

Lauren was at his mercy.

Alex made her feel like she was the most precious person in the world, treasured and loved. His hands trailed from her breasts, splayed across her abdomen, and slid over her hips along her thighs, weaving a spell of love transfixing her with passion.

"So beautiful," he rasped as he explored her body with tenderness.

Fate brought her to him, but the promise of love made her want to stay. He filled the air she breathed, kindling a new awareness of him in her heart, mind, and soul. He pleasured her with showers of desire, deliberately taking his time making her beg for more until her mind and body exploded with constant, pulsating aftershocks. Her head rocked back into the pillow as she screamed his name.

No more pretense. Just the need to have Alex inside of her. The look of love shining on his face squeezed her heart tight. "Make love to me, Alex."

He shifted her knees apart, their eyes met, and she knew the love exchanged between them was real, complete. Their tongues entwined with tantalizing kisses. Their breathing changed with every thrust. She loved the feel of her legs wrapped around his hips as she writhed in ecstasy. The more love he gave her— the more her affection multiplied in the euphoria of his passion—his inner light bursting forth, intoxicating her mind.

Breathing hard and fast, she arched to meet his rhythmic movements. Their eyes remained locked on each other with such intensity it made her dizzy. He drank her in and scooped her up.

Lauren reached up and touched his face. "I need you, Alex. I want you." Her words kicked in his primal need for connection. His love was pure, and she would cherish him.

After the snowstorm, Mason pulled out of Hall's Haven development and called the Colonel. "Hey, I'm calling the brothers. We're ready to move. I just got a call from the insurance agent. He's in town and making a house trip."

The Colonel replied, "Finally, good news. We'll meet after hours at The Dirty Rat to plan our exit strategy."

"See you later." Mason ended the call.

The ten-million-dollar life insurance policy on Bratten had been issued after he added Mason to the LLC. Six months later, Rose had Bratten unknowingly sign a change in beneficiary. Instead of the proceeds going to Lauren, the payout went to Mason.

In the beginning, Mason had no intention of cashing in on the policy as long as the limited liability company posed as the front for The RB's main cash cow. He and his brothers worked out a thing of beauty. If you had the money, you had the potential to buy and sell almost anything. Significant amounts of money came from the cartels for arms and an unlimited source of cheap labor.

The RB had offshore accounts in the Caymans, Bermuda, and the Bahamas, with homes in each locales and a villa in Mexico.

Mason drove along the back streets from Drake Properties, formulating a plan. He had to act quickly.

In a matter of hours, he needed to deactivate his local emails, bank accounts, and credit cards and discard their cell phones by removing the batteries, destroying the sims, and leaving the phones' shells at the bus station. Someone would steal the phones and help with the disinformation for the authorities.

The most significant hurdle was to wipe the primary drive and remote server from Drake Properties. He'd have to wait until the last hours in town before deleting the files. Then he'd boil the primary hard drive and smash it with a sledgehammer. Afterward, he'd run an electromagnetic wand to obliterate any data left.

Rose may be a problem. He intended on sending little Andre to his grandparents. Rose wouldn't want to leave the kid behind, but it was the best way to keep her safe. Plus, living on the lam wasn't a life for a child, and taking him would increase their chances of getting caught.

After filling out the forms, the insurance agent would enter the check online using Mason's routing and check number to the bank in the Caymans; then, he'd meet the brothers at the pub. They'd brainstorm how to best get out of the country, preferably to separate ports of call. They'd meet up later at the villa in Mexico at a specified date and time.

Mason breathed more comfortably with a plan percolating in his brain as he pulled into the garage and clicked the remote to shut the door. The Eagle Creek mission neared completion.

Rose cooked dinner while little Andre colored at the kitchen table inside the house. He circled her waist and kissed her neck. "You smell good enough to eat."

Rose shooed him away. "You don't want me to burn the chops, do you?"

He glanced at the boy and smacked Rose from behind. "Later, Ms. Rose. Someone is stopping by in a few minutes. Keep the boy in the kitchen. You two go ahead and eat without me. You can keep my plate warm in the microwave for later."

Placing her hand on her hip, she huffed, "Can't you do meetings at the office? Why at home? You know how important family meals are to me."

"The insurance agent is on the way here."

Rose's eyes went wide with surprise. "Does that mean what I think it does?"

"I certainly hope so. This chapter in our book of life is almost closed. You may want to send little Andre to his grand-parents for a few days. It will get crazy around here, and I need you sharp and not distracted, okay?"

"I guess he could stay for a few days. I'll call after dinner."

"I'm going to take a quick shower."

"Okay, want a beer?"

"I'll wait until our guest arrives." He chuckled.

Mason wore an untucked blue shirt over jeans and slid on a pair of loafers. Looking in the mirror, he smiled. He had sacrificed much, but soon, he and Rose would be living in a tropical paradise set for life.

Mason stepped out of the main suite. The insurance agent chatted with Rose, and little Andre played cars at her feet. He frowned at Rose, and she picked up the boy and went back into the kitchen, closing the door behind her.

"Hello, Shane. Did you have any trouble flying in?"

Shane stood and shook Mason's hand. "Not coming in, but I may be grounded if the snow keeps up."

Mason waved him to sit down. "Would you like a beer or a drink?"

Shane shook his head. "No. I better not. I have some forms for you to fill out before entering the check into your account. It took an enormous amount of time to get the check issued." Shane reached into his leather pouch, pulled out a black smart tablet, tapped with his stylus, and handed the tablet to Mason. "You need to read, sign, and date at the bottom of the screen."

Mason quickly reviewed the forms. By the time Shane left the house, he had thought the check would be in the RB Cayman account. He signed and dated each page, then gave the tablet back to Shane. "I guess you made a sizeable commission on this chunk of change."

Shane nodded. "Yeah. I won't lie. It was pretty sweet and catapulted me into the top agent slot a couple of years ago. I need your routing and account number."

Mason said, "I prefer to enter the numbers if you don't mind."

Shane handed the tablet back to Mason. "Click through the yes boxes until you get to the section to enter your routing and account number. Green checkmarks will illuminate the screen when entered correctly, scroll to the bottom of the screen, accept the terms, and click finish."

Mason followed the instructions and sighed when the money went through to the bank. The brothers made a lot of money, but ten million was the most significant one-time hit. "Give me a second to check my bank account to see if the transaction transferred." Mason grabbed his iPad and clicked the bank app. The money was in the bank. "Looks like all the zeros hit in the right places. Hey, we're getting ready to eat dinner. You're more than welcome to join us."

Shane wiped the palms of his hands on his pants. "No, no. That's okay. I have friends in town I'm visiting that I haven't seen in years." He stood and said, "Let me know if I may be of further assistance."

Mason tilted his head. Something niggled his brain. "Who're your friends? Maybe I know them."

Shane swallowed hard.

The man feared him. Mason sensed fear from a mile away.

"Oh, pretty sure you don't. Well, good to finally meet you. Best wishes." Shane made for the door, put on his coat and hat, then left.

Mason shrugged.

Why should he care about Shane's friends?

There were two types of rich: people with money and wealth. He'd just become a wealthy man.

He went into the kitchen with his iPad. "See, I told you to trust me. I told you that I'd take care of you and the boy."

Rose's eyes filled with tears. "I'm happy you have the money, but I hate how you got it. Bratten was a nice man."

Mason backhanded her in the mouth. "You would rather get Bratten's sloppy seconds than my first fruits. I did this for us, for you and the boy."

Rose cowered in fear.

Mason pulled her up into his arms. "I wish you wouldn't make me mad. I hate hitting you. You know I can't control my anger." He glanced down, and little Andre had crawled under the coffee table.

Mason's voice softened, "I'm sorry, son. I am trying to stop. I love your mother; I love you."

Little Andre stuck his thumb in his mouth.

"Come on out, Andre. Come to me, my son." The little boy crawled out and wrapped his arms around his mother's leg.

Rose said, "It's time for Andre's bath."

Mason grabbed her chin. "Forgive me, Rose."

Her lashes lowered, and she whispered, "I forgive you." She picked up Andre and went upstairs.

He hated himself. Rose was a good woman, and he would blow it if he didn't rein in his temper.

Chapter 11

Angeline rose from the sofa to greet Eron's guest. "Hello."

Eron draped an arm around his wife's shoulder. "Angeline, this is Shane. We played football together back in high school. He moved to New York a few years back."

Angeline shook his hand. "Nice to meet you, Shane. Eron and I were having a cocktail. Would you like beer or whiskey?"

Shane seemed nervous. "Would I? Whiskey and coke if you got it. You wouldn't believe the night I've had. I flew down in a winter storm to personally deliver a sizable claim to a client that makes me jumpy. I'm not supposed to discuss it, but rumor has it he's a hitman. He called my company a couple of years ago, and I was assigned his account. Huge money, don't get me wrong. But something about him stinks."

Angeline handed him his drink and sat on the couch, crossing her feet at the ankles. "Well, you've come to the right place. We love juicy gossip." She giggled.

Eron joined her on the couch. "We're glad to have you spend the night. I want to catch up, shoot the breeze and maybe play a game of pool later. The twins are in the bonus room watching movies or playing video games. Sit, take a load off."

"Thanks." Shane sat on the loveseat next to the sofa. "Man, I'm glad you answered your phone today, or I'd be stuck in a motel next to the airport."

"Not a problem, buddy," replied Eron.

Angeline sipped her drink. "Tell us about this fascinating client of yours. It sounds like something you'd see at the movies."

Shane unbuttoned his jacket and leaned back against the sofa. "The man served in the Middle East, but I don't think he served with any branch of our government military. He worked for a private company. Scary dude."

Eron said, "Shane, you don't have to talk about it."

"No, man. It's over for me, thank god. Hopefully, I'll never hear from him again."

Angeline sat her drink on a coaster. "So, what's the client's name. We may know him."

Eron frowned. "Angeline, you're not supposed to ask questions like that."

"Why not?"

Shane waved his hand. "No, it's all right. I almost didn't get the check issued in the first place. What I'm about you tell you has to stay between us, or I could lose my job. The initial policy covered both partners, but one of them died last year. Um, the partner was murdered, but no one's been arrested. The company did an in-depth investigation before cutting the check."

Angeline stiffened. "What was the name of the partner that died?" Her fingernails bit into her palms.

Shane took a sip of his drink. "Bratten Drake. Know him?"

Angeline's cheeks flushed red. She choked out, "Bratten Drake was married to my sister."

The color drained from Shane's face. "What?"

Eron said, "Yeah, man, Bratten was our brother-in-law. A fine man. Mason, that son of a bitch."

"Oh my god. Mason just deposited a ten-million-dollar payout from my company. I feel sick." He gulped the whiskey.

Angeline screamed, "Ten million dollars? I have to call Lauren."

Shane jumped to his feet and shouted, "No, you can't. I'll get fired. I'll lose my license. I have a family to support."

"Tough shit! My brother-in-law was killed, and he had a family too," said Angeline.

Eron looked at Angeline and squeezed her hand. "Breathe, baby, settle down. Shane, we don't want you to get fired, but many crimes have been committed against our family, and we think Mason Williams is responsible. I'm calling the police. Ten million dollars gives Mason a huge motive."

Angeline drank the rest of her cocktail. "I have Detective Stone's business card. Should I call Lauren?"

Eron looked at his watch. "It's late. Let's wait until I talk with the police before we alarm her."

Shane went paper pale, swiping his hand across his forehead. "I'm so sorry. I'm at a loss. I don't know what to say."

Angeline glared at Shane, then let loose on the man. "You knew the partner was murdered and still issued the check. A ten million dollar check. Who do you think killed him? The janitor? Huge money, indeed. More like blood money. How do you sleep at night?" She looked at Eron and asked, "And why wouldn't Alex know about a large policy?"

Eron stepped into the kitchen and called Detective Stone, relaying the information. A few minutes later, he walked back into the room. "The information is with the authorities. Detective Stone said he'd contact Lauren as soon as he received the warrant for Mason's arrest. With the weather, it may be tomorrow before he can secure one. He doesn't want to place Lauren in any more danger, so we'll sit on it tonight."

Eron pulled Angeline into his arms, rubbing her back. "Baby, if Shane hadn't come over tonight, the police wouldn't be seeking an arrest warrant."

Shane said, "Look, I'll leave. I am sorry, Angeline. You're right, the company did an investigation, but legally they had to release the check. If Mason is responsible, they will seek damages."

"Don't leave Shane. The weather is bad. Without your information, Mason could've gotten away with murder. Right, Angeline?"

Angeline let out a exhale. "I guess you're right. I'm sorry for biting your head off. Why don't you and Eron catch up? I'm going to check on the kids, and then I'm going to bed." She kissed Eron. "I'm calling Lauren. She would want to know."

Angeline poured a glass of wine and made her way to the bonus room to check on the twins. They were engrossed in the Mario Party video game. She kissed each of them and said, "I love you."

"Mom, we love you too. But please...." Brenda looked around her mom while maneuvering the controller.

She smiled. "Okay, you have thirty more minutes, then brush your teeth and get in bed."

"Okay, we promise." Jenny hugged her.

Angeline went into her bedroom and closed the door. She placed her wine on the nightstand and put a call to Lauren, and it went to voicemail. Angeline didn't leave a message. She'd call Lauren first thing in the morning.

Chapter 12

Lauren drove to Drake Properties before sunrise for an early meeting. Another round of snow showers was heading in midmorning from the radar report, and she wanted to select the custom street lighting for Wycliffe Avenue. Then she'd go back home to Alex.

Lauren kept thinking about Alex and Bratten. The similarities and the differences. Overall, they were the best two people she'd ever met, and she loved them both. She hadn't called Bratten's name because she wasn't ready to tell him her feelings.

She whipped into her parking space in front of Drake Properties and turned off her car. Lauren emailed the employees last night that they could work from home. The roads were still dangerous from the first snow, and the next storm would make driving treacherous.

Sunrise wouldn't come for another hour, so the streetlights cast long shadows across the front entrance. She grabbed her laptop bag and exited the vehicle. Clean Sweep must've cleared the parking lot, sidewalks, and front steps of ice and snow.

The faint howl made the hair on her arms and neck bristle. In the distance, the chug of a freight train rolled over the tracks.

The meeting with O'Reilly Lighting and Supply house rep had been pushed back twice, and she didn't want to hold up the project with a custom order. The representative would arrive in about forty-five minutes, which gave her enough time to review the online catalog one last time. She'd picked out a couple of designs she liked for the street lamps. The meeting wouldn't last long if the vendor came in with the price.

Lauren keyed in the code and walked into the office. She went about turning on lights and, all the while, smiling, reminiscing about Alex.

A loud banging and crash startled her. She reached for her phone and sent Alex a text.

Lauren: Alex, someone is in the IT Department. Call the police.

She grabbed Bratten's nine iron next to the couch and crept down the hallway. Gripping the golf club, she tiptoed toward the IT department.

Mason slung the door open. His face distorted with a menacing quality sending her creep meter from high alert to DEF-CON five, kicking in her flight or fight adrenaline. Prickles of fear rose within her chest. The computer equipment behind him was destroyed.

Mason gave Lauren a smirk. "Hey, partner. You're at work early. Too bad for you."

Lauren held the club and shouted, "Stay back. I swear, Mason, I can swing a club."

Mason threw a hammer at her head with lightning speed, knocking her off her feet. She thought of Alex before slipping into unconsciousness.

Curses flew out of Mason's mouth. He threw Lauren's cell phone into the IT room, then scooped her into his arms and ran out of the rear entrance into the back parking lot, placing her in the back seat of his vehicle.

Mason reached into his pant pocket, pulled out his cell, removed the battery, and stomped on his phone before hurling it into Harold's Grocery's backlot. He got in the truck, punched the ignition, and floored the accelerator. He heard the police sirens pulling into what he assumed was Drake Properties two streets over.

Mason punched the dashboard while racing to the farm. He opened the console, grabbed an untraceable phone, and plugged it into the charger before calling T-bone's number. "We have a situation. Get Rose's boy to his grandmother's and bring Rose to the safe house. We're leaving the country tonight." Whipping wind and snow swirled against his windshield.

Forty minutes later, Mason turned onto the private road to the farm. He glanced at Lauren in the back seat.

Should he kill her or take her with them?

He placed the truck in park and jumped out. He ran and opened the sliding doors to the barn. Jumping back into the vehicle, he pulled it inside and then turned off the truck's engine. He slid out of the Tundra and shut the barn door.

Mason swept the hay aside inside the last stall and opened a trap door. He reached into the back seat and threw Lauren over his shoulder, taking her down the stepladder to an underground storm cellar.

The cellar had a small pantry, a living area with a twin bed and couch, and a bathroom with only a toilet and sink. Mason had added electricity, plumbing, and a ventilation system. No sound, and the temperature stayed a steady sixty-four degrees year-round.

Mason hoisted Lauren onto the bed, strapping her arms to the rails, then waited until she regained consciousness.

Blood oozed from the gash in Lauren's hairline. She needed stitches.

Decisions. Decisions.

Part of him knew he should kill her and dispose of the body. Part of him wanted to keep her.

It could be afternoon before T-bone lost the cops and headed to the farm. Mason went into the pantry and pulled out a syringe of diamorphine, and gave Lauren an injection. He had stockpiles of pain meds from his contacts over the border. He learned over the years that killing with meds left little mess and was harder to trace.

Lauren moaned and blinked her eyes. She jerked on the restraints, but the meds would work soon.

He stared at her. "Hey, Lauren."

"What have you done? Where am I?" her voice strained.

Mason's fingers tingled with excitement. "You're in a secure location. Scream until you lose your voice, but no one will hear you. No one."

"You won't get away with this, Mason." Her words thickened as she jerked her arms again. "Rose knows that you killed her husband."

"You don't know what the hell you're talking about. I didn't kill Andre. He was my friend."

Lauren's eyes rolled, and she tried lifting her head. "I found the letter from Andre. He told you he was leaving the brotherhood, and you killed him just like you killed Bratten."

Mason sat down and leaned his chin on the top of the chair rail. "As I said, I didn't kill Andre. You have no idea what we went through over there. We had to stick together because you never knew if each day was your last. We couldn't tell the enemy from the good guys because there were no good guys where we were stationed. IEDs, drone strikes, it was kill or be killed. Andre knew what he signed on for, and I told him not to leave. Why do you think I married Rose?"

Lauren's lids fluttered. "You married Rose?"

"Yes, I married Rose to protect her and Andre's son. They would've taken them over the border and sold them. Wake up, Girl Scout, the world isn't *Big Little Lies*. It's Armageddon."

"Why Bratten? Why?"

"Bratten knew too much, and he should've stayed away from Rose."

Lauren spat at him, and he wiped it from his face, then backhanded her hard. "Look, Mrs. Drake, I get off on inflicting pain. If you make me hit you again, you'll suffer." He got off on receiving pain too.

"Demented sadist."

Mason punched her in the gut. "Yeah? No doubt. See what you made me do. Can't breathe, can you? Do you want some more?" He smoothed her hair and gripped her face. "Don't move a muscle." He watched the fear grow in her eyes, and he wanted to take her bad but couldn't lose focus with so much shit going down. He crushed her with a bruising kiss drawing blood from her lips. "Hm. Good."

"Don't. Don't do this to me." Lauren stilled as the meds kicked in.

"Nightie night, Princess."

Bratten watched helplessly as Mason hit Lauren, disrespecting and degrading her. He screamed so loud that St. Peter himself must've heard. He tried punching Mason repeatedly, crying, "You bastard," and never made contact.

He thought about taking over Mason, but the man's soul was dark, and there was a chance he could lose his soul in the process.

He floated through the barn and watched Mason walk inside the farmhouse.

Bratten closed his eyes and thought of his headstone. In milliseconds, he appeared in the cemetery.

Dark clouds blanketed the sky, masking the sun against the gravestones. A misty fog thickened around him as the snow fell in sheets.

Bratten looked up into the snow-covered trees. The branches rustled as a flock of black crows flew away. There was an old saying about crows foreshadowing death. Anywhere crows gathered, the dead waited and watched. He walked along the deserted path looking for spirits willing to help him.

A cold breeze swirled around him.

"Why have you come, Bratten Drake?"

Bratten said, "I can't see you." A sudden force pushed him to the ground on his knees. Bratten cried, "Show me how you did that?"

"What?" the spirit voice seemed puzzled. "Why? Do you want to haunt someone's dreams?"

Bratten came to his feet and shouted, "No. I want to kill someone."

Laughter and shouts roared through the cemetery, and dozens of spirits surrounded him, chanting, "Join us, Bratten."

Bratten felt a mighty presence but couldn't see the spirit that asked the question.

"An evil man holds my wife hostage in a cellar not far from this place. I must free her and kill the man before it's too late," pleaded Bratten.

The presence materialized in battle armor with sunken eyes and a slackened jaw. "If you take a human life, your soul will be doomed for eternity."

"I will give my soul to save my wife."

Shrieks and shouts rang out, "Kill the man. Kill the beast. We know the man that you seek."

"Follow me, Bratten Drake. I will show you how to inflict pain. I will show you how to save your wife."

Bratten followed him past intricately carved headstones toward the oldest part of the cemetery inside an impressive classical-styled mausoleum with ornate designs.

Inside the chamber, the warrior said, "You are a spirit in the world of the living. The only skill you have left is visualization.

You must hone those skills to move any objects. Let's say a padlock."

The warrior glided over to the steel bars with an antique padlock. "If you want to open the lock, you must be the lock. You must be every nuance of the lock, the smell of the rust, and the mechanisms that move inside and unlock it." The warrior disappeared, and in less than a second, the padlock opened and fell to the ground.

Bratten said, "Yes, I want to learn how to do that."

The warrior said, "Channel your energies into the lock. Focus on nothing but picking up the lock and securing it back to the gate."

The warrior dematerialized into a spirit wind and swirled around Bratten.

"Practice, Bratten Drake. Once you've placed the lock back on the bars, we'll move to the living."

Chapter 13

Alex received two texts almost simultaneously.

Angeline: I've been trying to reach Lauren. No answer. Mason received a ten-million-dollar payout yesterday on a life insurance policy he took out on Bratten. Help!

Lauren: Someone is in the IT Department. Call the police.

Alex ran out the back door and jumped into his SUV while calling Detective Stone and Logan Clarkson. He relayed the texts and said he'd meet them at Drake Properties.

He called Angeline, and she answered right away.

"Alex? Is Lauren with you?"

"No, she went to the office early this morning for a meeting. Her phone is going straight to voicemail. I'm on my way to her office now. I'll call as soon as I learn something." Alex released an exhale.

Alex opened the glove box, pulled out a .45 Glock Automatic, and then grabbed a couple of cartridges. Alex punched the dashboard several times. He should've gone with Lauren to work this morning, but she declined the offer. Lauren was a hardheaded, independent woman. He loved and hated that about her.

By the time Alex reached Drake Properties, several squad cars had surrounded the place. Lauren's SUV was parked out front. SWAT members exited their vehicles, heading to the front, side, and backdoors.

Logan wore an FBI coat.

Alex ran over and yelled, "FBI? Are you kidding? Agent Logan, where is Lauren?"

Logan said, "We just got here. Sorry, Alex, I couldn't tell you I was working undercover. My team's been tracking Mason and his brothers for several years. We've never had enough information to arrest him until now, so you need to stay put."

"The hell you say. I'm going in."

Logan held Alex's arm. "Wait a minute. You don't want to get her killed, do you?"

Detective Stone yelled, "Police." He entered the building.

Officers poured into Drake Properties with weapons drawn. Shouts rang out, "Police. Clear. Police. Clear."

Through gritted teeth, Alex said, "I'm going to kill him if he's laid one hand on her."

Logan said, "Son, don't do anything stupid."

"Don't call me, son."

After what seemed like an eternity, Detective Stone approached Alex and Logan. With a grim expression, he said, "Lauren's gone. Her purse, laptop, and phone are inside."

Alex dropped to his knees and screamed. "God, no."

Mason had killed Bratten, and he had Lauren.

Logan placed his hand out and helped Alex up. "We have special agents on the way to Mason's, and we've notified the air traffic controller. Flights are grounded due to the weather. No one is leaving town."

Detective Stone said, "I have to wrap up here. Call me, Logan, if you hear anything." He went back into Drake Properties.

Alex looked at Logan and said, "Either you let me come with you, or I'll search for her myself. Drake Properties owns warehouses and tracts of land all over the county."

"I'm aware. We're searching, Alex."

Alex shouted at Logan. "Why wouldn't you warn her? Warn me? I could've kept her from going to work even if I had to sit on her."

"You can ride with me, Alex, but you're not carrying that weapon, and some of the information is classified, so I may or may not answer you."

"Oh, yes, I am, Mr. FBI. I have a permit to carry a weapon."

"Look, Alex, I won't apologize for doing my job. I can't worry about protecting you while I'm in pursuit of dangerous criminals."

Alex pressed his lips into a firm line. "I am coming with you freely and won't hold the FBI responsible if I get hurt or killed. I can create one online while we get in your damn truck and drive."

Alex wanted vengeance.

He wanted Mason's blood.

Alex didn't think about the consequences; he wanted to beat Mason senseless.

Bratten quickly developed the telekinesis skills to move and manipulate objects, then he thought of the private investigator, Logan Clarkson. He closed his eyes and appeared in his double cab truck, and Logan nearly drove off the road.

Alex sat up front and yelled, "Watch out."

"Alex, I know where Mason's holding Lauren, but we must hurry," said Bratten.

Logan gripped the steering wheel of his SUV and glanced in the rearview mirror. "Good granny grunts, I'm losing my mind."

"No, Logan, I'm real. Tell him, Alex. We're going to Mason's farm. That's where he has Lauren."

Alex said, "Believe me, he's real."

The brisk wind blew sheets of snowflakes into Logan's line of sight as he let up on the gas pedal, but the truck hit black ice spinning out of control, crashing into a guardrail, then went airborne into a ravine.

Logan groaned and looked at Alex. He was unconscious.

Logan grabbed his phone and dialed 9-1-1. "Dag-nab-it, no cell service. I'll radio in and pray the enemy doesn't intercept. How close are we to the farm?"

Bratten clenched and unclenched his fists. "Three or four miles, at least. She's locked in a storm cellar inside the barn of the old place."

He pressed the button and said, "Akio. Do you read me? Akio?"

"Yes. I read you."

"I flipped my truck turning onto Mills Pond Road, south-bound. I'm going to try and shift into two-wheel drive. If that doesn't work, Alex and I are heading on foot. We need backup and first responders asap. Look for an old barn and farmhouse."

Akio replied, "Got it. Our team is en route. I'm keying in your coordinates and mapping the satellite image. I'll track your movements."

"Thanks, Akio."

There wasn't a car in sight on Mills Pond Road in either direction. Logan turned up the defrost. "I can't see two feet in front of my face." He pushed Alex's arm. "Man, are you all right?"

Alex moaned, "What happened?"

"We're in a ditch. Hold on." Logan gunned the gas, but the tires kept spinning. Logan glanced in the back seat. "Well, bull roar. Grab one of the coats in the back. We're going to hoof it."

"What about your phone?" Alex asked.

"No service. I radioed my team. Barring other accidents, the backup should arrive when we need them."

Logan frowned. "Here, you need a vest. How many cartridges do you have?"

"Two." Alex grabbed the vest and FBI coat. "Let's rock."

Logan grunted.

Entering the farmhouse, Mason called out, "Juan, Diago?" No answer.

He threw several sticks of wood onto the hearth. "Damn it. Don't I have enough problems?" He started a fire and put on a pot of coffee. He walked to the front door watching the snowfall. He tried using his safety net phone to no avail. He had no clue if T-bone was en route to the farm with Rose or busted.

Mason finished his cup of coffee and placed the mug in the sink. He pulled on his coat and hat to look for Juan and Diago, then he'd check on Lauren.

Walking along the back of the property, it didn't take long for him to find the two young men covered in snow with bullet wounds to their heads. He looked around for weapons and found none. Damn it. Esteban would have someone's head, and it wouldn't be his.

The wintry mix and whipping wind penetrated his coat and hat. His fingers and feet were freezing by the time he entered the barn's back door.

He opened the cellar door. Stepping down the ladder, Mason heard Lauren crying. God, he hated when women cried.

Lauren blinked several times and pressed her lips together.

"Are you hungry? Do you need to go to the bathroom?"

Through gritted teeth, she said, "It's a little hard to pee when I'm chained to the bed."

Mason reached into his coat pocket and pulled out the key. "A warning. You try to escape; I'll kill you."

"Where's Juan?" she asked.

"Dead."

She gasped. "You monster. What did Juan ever do to you?"

Mason could tell Lauren he didn't kill Juan, but he wanted her afraid. Captives tended to do what they're told when frightened. "Do we understand each other?"

She lowered her voice, "Yes, I understand."

He waited next to the bathroom door and ran over different scenarios. He didn't worry about the local cops, but the TBI and Feds could cause the RB significant problems. Thankfully, a couple of weeks ago, Dennis moved the jet from the Drake Properties private hangar to an industrial hangar away from the commercial airport.

Mason chuckled, thinking about the cops raiding the Drake hangar and finding nothing.

This ain't my first rodeo, boys.

The pending insurance check posted to the bank after midnight. He just had to get Rose and get to the plane.

Stepping out of the bathroom, Lauren shifted sideways so as not to rub next to him. She turned and faced him. "Don't chain me to the bed. I'm not going anywhere."

He leaned against the concrete wall. "You need stitches. I'm pretty decent at dressing field wounds and have a kit. Sit down."

She sat in the straight back chair, and her fingers closed into tight fists.

Mason noticed the slight tremor in her arms and the twitching of her feet, probably caused by fear and the drugs.

He opened the pantry and pulled out the locked medicine box. "Tilt your head back." She did, and he used a medicine dropper to cleanse the wound with a saline solution and then alcohol.

Lauren winced in pain, biting her swollen lip, but she didn't scream.

It took about twenty minutes to stitch and dress the wound. Mason filled another syringe with painkillers.

Lauren looked sick. "No more drugs, please."

"It's a mild pain reliever. You may get a little dizzy, but it won't knock you out. I'm afraid you're going to have a scar on your hairline. Not sure your hair will grow back." He locked the box and returned it to the pantry. "I'm expecting some people. There's food in the pantry." He gave her the shot in her arm.

"Are you completely insane? You hit me in the head with a hammer, and you're worried if I will have a scar?" she asked.

"Yeah, I'm crazy. Insane? Probably. Are you afraid to die?"

She lifted her chin and defiantly shouted, "I welcome death."

His chin dipped to his chest. "No more crying? No begging or pleading for mercy?"

"I won't beg for my life." She straightened her back and said, "The crying you heard was for my family and Alex, not myself. How did you kill Bratten? Did he know you betrayed him? Boy, you had us fooled. We both trusted you."

He ignored her question. "Ah, yes, the suffering Alex, torn between the love of a friend or you. No brainer, I knew he'd pick you. I'd do the same." He chuckled.

She teetered in the chair.

"Lie down either on the couch or sofa. If you'd just stayed home this morning, I'd be halfway out of the country. You and Alex would've been free to do whatever. Fate is a funny mistress."

She plopped onto the couch, falling asleep in seconds.

Lauren woke with a throbbing headache, shivering from the cold and an overpowering scent of dank earth. She reached up and remembered the hammer striking her head and the stitches. "Ow." She groggily came to an upright position placing her feet on the cold, rough cement floor.

She took in her surroundings. The cellar was made of concrete blocks and mildewed walls painted white with the flickering fluorescent lights and old copper piping overhead. The tiny room caused her to panic. The walls seemed to close in, making her sway with dizziness.

Lauren climbed the old rusty metal ladder screwed into the wall on the far-right side of the room. Lauren pushed with all her might, but the door didn't budge. She pounded with her fists and screamed, "Let me out of here, you son of a bitch."

Minutes seemed to last for hours. No sound from the other side and no noise from underground. Her mouth was bone dry with a metallic taste, and her throat hurt. She stepped down the ladder and surveyed the area. She was looking for anything that she could use as a weapon.

She pulled the light fixture cord inside the pantry, revealing rows of canned food items and drinks. She grabbed a soda and popped the top, and greedily drank its contents.

The small bathroom had a white porcelain sink and toilet that'd seen better days. There were no clocks, phones, or windows and no way to tell if it was day or night.

Mason's drugs made Lauren unstable on her feet. She tried to calm shattered nerves but being locked in an underground cellar made her hyperventilate. She sat on a metal chair and took slow breaths in and out until the panic attack subsided.

Lauren rifled through every shelf in the small storage room and found Mason's locked box. She took one of the canned food items, held the package between her legs, and pounded the lock until she finally knocked it off. Inside were vials of medicine and syringes along with first-aid items.

Was Mason a drug dealer?

She wondered how much time before Mason returned to finish the job.

Was he going to kill her?

Her heart pounded, and her pulse raced, but she wasn't going down without a fight.

Lauren filled a few syringes and placed one under the pillow, one under the hard mattress, and one on the plaid couch cushion, the last one in the bathroom behind the door.

If Mason didn't shoot her, she might have a chance to juice him.

Fearing for her life, the tears rolled off her cheeks. She'd been a fool. She should've never gone to work at Drake Properties. She thought of Bratten and cried some more.

"Bratten? Can you hear me? Bratten, can you see me?"

Lauren pressed the palms of her hands into her eyes. She had taken so much in her life for granted. Lauren wished she could go back in time to tell Bratten every day what a miracle he'd been in her life. She would've loved him like each second was their last.

Lauren would've told her parents every day she loved them. Work often to precedence over quality time with her family. She wished she'd spent more time with Angeline and her family.

Alex. She should've told him she loved him when she had the chance.

She placed her hand gingerly on her forehead. Her mind played tricks on her.

"Bratten?"

He materialized before her. Dropping to his knees, he said, "Darling, what has he done to you?"

She ran her fingers through his hair. "Mason hit me in the head with a hammer and locked me down in this hole. Can you get me out of here, please?"

Bratten's spirit seemed to have corporeal properties. He came to his feet and caressed her cheek. "Mason will pay for hurting you. I've acquired some new telekinesis skills. Let's get you out of here."

Her hand went to her throat. "Someone's coming."

"Logan and Alex are on their way. It's snowing again, and the roads are bad, but they're coming."

Mason opened the trap door. He held a gun in his hand as he descended the ladder. "Who are you talking to?" He frantically looked around as she looked at Bratten.

Bratten glided over to her.

Lauren didn't say anything. She clenched her jaw and edged her way to the couch where she'd hidden a syringe.

Mason waved the gun in the air. "Answer me, or so help me, God, I'll shoot you."

Bratten punched Mason in the face. "You, son of a bitch."

Mason said, "What the hell?"

Bratten punched him again.

Mason stumbled back against the ladder. His face paled. "What the hell is going on?"

Lauren laughed hysterically. "You have one pissed ghost on your hands, and he's going to kick your sorry ass."

Mason rushed Lauren, but Bratten barreled him into the wall knocking the gun out of his hands. Mason scrambled to his feet and grabbed the gun.

With an edge of sarcasm, Lauren said, "You remember my husband, Bratten Drake. He's returned for a little payback."

Mason pulled back the hammer, the gun aimed at Lauren. "I'll shoot her. I swear I will." He backed up the ladder and slammed the trap door shut.

Bratten melted through the trap door and punched Mason in the mouth. "You touch my wife again, and you'll be six feet under in Everpine Cemetery."

Mason looked around, not seeing him. "Is it you, Bratten?"

"You killed me for money? You took my life for greed?" Bratten kicked Mason in the balls, and he doubled over.

Mason growled. "You touch me again, and I'll burn the barn to the ground. You and Lauren can have a proper reunion. I swear, Bratten." He inched over to a can of gasoline. "One shot, and the place will go up in flames with all the straw and hay. Crates of ammo and guns will explode like the Fourth of freakin' July.

Bratten roared. He didn't know how to put out a fire. He dematerialized to Logan and Alex climbing out of the ditch. "Hurry. Mason's going to kill her. Go three miles and take a right down a tractor lane. It'll take you to that white farmhouse and a barn you almost bought, Alex. Lauren's held inside the barn in an underground cellar. I'm going back. I won't leave her again." He faded away.

Chapter 14

Out of breath, Mason ran back to the house. Slipping and falling several times before he reached the front door. Mason didn't believe in ghosts, but Bratten's spirit kicked the shit out of him. Bruises and swelling appeared on his face as he looked into the bathroom mirror.

Scratching his head, Mason strode into the kitchen and pulled out a bottle of whiskey. He rarely drank but needed a shot because the episode with Bratten was something out of a horror flick. You couldn't kill someone already dead.

Mason's quick thinking, threatening Lauren's life with fire, backed the ghost off.

What was he waiting on? Why didn't he just go ahead and shoot Lauren?

He heard a car engine revved outside. He looked out the door, and T-bone and Rose parked in the drive next to the side of the house.

Reinforcements.

How could Mason tell T-bone that a ghost kicked his ass? He'd think Mason lost his mind. Maybe he had.

He opened the door, and Rose ran into his arms.

"Oh, Mason. I'm so scared."

He wrapped his arms around her tight and looked at T-bone. "Were you followed?"

"No, but two FBI agents wrecked a few miles back, and they're walking in this direction. The Colonel's coming too."

"Son of a bitch. What else is going to go wrong?"

They sat down at the kitchen table. "There's no cell service. Did you contact Dennis to get the jet ready?"

T-bone extended his legs and stretched. "Yeah, but air traffic canceled all flights for tonight."

"Great. Perfect." Mason scratched his neck and told them about Lauren.

Rose gasped. "Stitches? She could have a concussion. Mason, you can't keep her locked underground."

"Too freaking bad, that's where she's staying. You understand that you'll go to prison if we're caught."

"Yes, I understand. But, Mason, I can't allow you...."

He backhanded her. "Shut up the hell up. I have enough problems without listening to you go on about Lauren. Depending on the Colonel, I'm thinking about taking her on as a mistress. Still, want to embrace your new sister wife?"

Rose stormed out of the room into the bedroom, slamming the door.

T-bone sat with his arms crossed over his chest. "Give Lauren to me. I've wanted to taste that piece of ass since she danced at The Dirty Rat."

Mason tilted his head and glared. "She's outta of your league, bro. Get with the program, man. We have to get out of the country, and then we'll see who she prefers."

T-bone chuckled, placed two fingers over his mouth, and did disgusting things with his tongue. "She'll beg for this lashing."

Mason frowned, narrowing his eyes at T-bone. "Did you kill Juan and Diago?"

T-bone shrugged. "They were trying to escape. Fast little suckers too."

"You can tell Esteban." Mason had a thought. He'd send T-bone to check on Lauren. He'd let the ghost of Bratten Drake kick the shit out of T-bone too. Mason wouldn't have to explain anything. He'd get everything under control before the Colonel arrived. No loose ends. "You can have Lauren, but don't leave visible marks."

T-bone grinned. "Gladly, boss." He left out the side door toward the barn.

Mason went to the bedroom and knocked softly. "Pumpkin, I'm sorry. Open the door for daddy." He heard sniffles. He hated when Rose cried. "Come on, baby."

Rose opened the door wiping her eyes with the back of her hand.

"Come kiss daddy. I gave Lauren to T-bone, okay?"

"Why are you so mean to me?"

Mason circled his arms around Rose's waist and drew her up in a kiss, slamming the door shut.

Lauren held the metal chair in her hands, ready to hit Mason, but someone else came down the steps. As the man neared the last rung on the ladder, Lauren slammed him in the back as hard as she could with the chair. He fell to the concrete floor. She'd seen him at The Dirty Rat. Midge called him T-bone.

His eyes widened and then narrowed. "Hellion, huh? I like my women crazy."

Lauren hit him on top of the head again and again until T-bone moved no longer.

Bratten placed his hands on her wrists. "He's out. Don't kill him. If anyone kills him, it's going to be me. Get the ties off the bed. We need to bind his wrists and ankles. Mason will come for him, and when he does, we'll be ready."

Lauren grabbed the ties and pulled them tight at T-bone's wrists and secured his ankles, then tore a piece of duct tape and placed it over his mouth.

With Bratten's help, she dragged T-bone into the corner of the room so that she could keep an eye on him.

She smacked T-bone twice across the face.

Bratten chuckled. "Who are you, and where's my wife?"

She turned and looked up at Bratten. "Am I your wife?"

Bratten plopped on the orange and yellow plaid couch. "Oh, Alex, I tried to forget about that. So, you and Alex are a thing?"

She sat down beside him and squeezed his hand. "Yes. I think so."

"I'm happy for you." He stood abruptly and kicked the bed. "No, I'm not, but hey, I'm dead."

"But you said if you could pick anyone, it'd be Alex. You said that love was limitless and held no bounds. Were you lying?"

Staring at her, he said, "No. I wasn't lying. I meant it at the time. I think part of me sensed the attraction between you and Alex. He's been in love with you forever. It's not fair, though. We were robbed of our life together, robbed of my two girls and one boy, two dogs, and maybe one cat. But I want you to survive the mess I made of things. I want you to have children, and maybe if you have a son, you can name him after me."

Tears rolled down Lauren's cheeks, and her breath caught. "How could Mason do this to you? To us? What kind of man does that?"

"The kind of man trained to kill. Killing holds no moral compass for Mason. Greed is his savior."

Lauren said, "I found a box of syringes with pain medicine. I made up a few and hid them around the cellar to use on Mason. I had no idea he'd send T-bone."

Bratten said, "Show me where you hid them. We may need to use them as weapons. I'd go and look, but I don't want to leave you down here with that animal."

She took Bratten around the room. "Is that enough?"

"It wouldn't hurt to make up a few more syringes just in case. Start with injecting that asshole."

Lauren stared at him and asked, "Is it scary?"

"What?"

"Dying."

He stopped and lifted her chin with his finger. "No. Confusion, at first. But I was never afraid. Love and peace-filled the white room. It's like a train station where people move from one destination to another. I had unfinished business here, so I didn't move on. The world is one messed up place. Life is fleeting and ends too quickly, but the afterlife isn't scary."

She sat back down on the couch and curled her feet under her legs. "I have a screaming migraine."

Bratten hovered. "Take something. Look in the med box and see if you can find an anti-inflammatory."

Lauren opened one eye and then the other. "So, if I die today, you'll be waiting?"

He lifted her hand and pressed a kiss. "You're not dying today. You'll live to a ripe old age with grandchildren and great-grandchildren, but when the time comes for you to crossover, I'll be waiting."

Detective Stone called Logan repeatedly, but the calls went straight to voicemail. Something must've happened. He felt it in his gut. Ray called the chief and said, "Hey, I have a lead I want to check out before sunset, then I'll head back to the station."

Chief Lee replied, "Go. Keep me in the loop."

Ray sent Pete to the Drake Hangar, then checked his weapons and cartridges and sped along the highway to Mills Pond Road.

Chapter 15

The wind blew swirling snow horizontally as Alex and Logan jogged onto the old tractor lane. Cedar boughs were heavy with ice and snow, and huge drifts made it challenging to see what lay under its blanket. Clouds covered most of the sky, waning in the remaining light of day.

Out of breath, Logan stood next to a row of trees and bushes. "Mason may have an army up there, so let's cut through the woods. It may take longer, but less likely we're seen."

Alex shivered. "Gotcha." His fingers and toes were numb climbing over the barbed wire fence. Alex lost his footing and fell into a deep ditch. "Watch out, Logan. That first step's steep."

Logan climbed over the fence and went knee-deep in powder. "Check your weapon."

Alex pulled the Glock out of his vest and released the safety. "Hey, I've been here before. I looked at this property a few years back. The barn's not too far from here. Hurry, Logan."

Logan said, "Stay low, Alex. Keep an eye out for tripwires or any movement. The element of surprise is the only thing on our side."

Alex ran into stumps and boulders hidden by the snow walking through the woods. Bushes and thorny limbs grabbed and pulled his clothing. He didn't care if he was black and blue and bleeding all over—Lauren needed him.

Within twenty minutes, the old red barn with a rusty tin roof came into view. Alex stopped and waited for Logan to catch up. "I didn't want to yell. Let's see if we can enter from the back of the barn."

Logan readied his weapon and moved in front of Alex. "Follow me. If you hear pops, hit the ground and find cover."

They inched closer to the barn.

"Watch me then replicate." Logan lowered and ran to the back of the barn, plastering himself against the back wall, then waved Alex in.

Alex's heart pounded as he ducked, running to the barn. "The storm cellar is on the left. Let me go in first, and you cover me."

Logan nodded, and they swiftly entered the barn.

It took Alex a minute to allow his eyes to adjust to the darkened interior. He raced to the last stall when he didn't see anyone in the barn. The cell door wasn't locked. He didn't wait on Logan and slung the door open, descending the steps. He caught the edge of a metal chair on the final step and whipped around.

Lauren gasped. "Alex? Oh, god, is it you?"

"Thank you, Jesus. You're alive." He did a quick once over and gritted his teeth. "You're hurt." He wrapped her up in his arms, then noticed the man in the corner bound at the ankles and wrist with silver duct tape over his mouth. "Who's that?"

"T-bone. He works for Mason." She hugged him tight and looked up into his eyes.

Alex wondered how Lauren captured T-bone but caught a glimpse of Bratten. "Is Mason inside the house?" he asked.

"I think so."

He took a deep breath and exhaled. "Come on, baby. Let's get you out of here."

"What about T-bone?"

"Leave him for the authorities. Hurry."

Alex watched Lauren climb the ladder, then followed behind her. Reaching the top step, Alex froze.

Mason had Lauren in a chokehold with one arm and held a gun pressed to her temple with his other hand. "Back off, lawyer boy, or I'll shoot her. So, stay back."

Alex raised his hands. "Don't hurt her." He didn't look around for Logan, just praying that he'd come to their rescue quickly.

Mason backed out of the barn dragging Lauren. "What happened to T-bone?"

Alex glared. He followed a few steps behind them. His temper rose to the point of erupting into a full-blown rage. His voice deepened, "Why don't you go into the cellar and find out?"

About thirty feet from the white farmhouse, Logan stepped behind Mason and shouted, "Drop your weapon. You're under arrest for the murder of Bratten Drake."

A police car raced toward them with flashing blue lights and screeching sirens. Coming to a stop, Detective Stone exited the ECP vehicle with his gun drawn. He shouted, "Drop your weapons."

Alex blinked the snow out of his eyes as Rose raced out of the front door with a semi-automatic rifle.

Rose screamed, "Lower your weapon, Colonel." She shouted, "Lauren, he killed Bratten, not Mason. He killed Andre too. He ordered a hit on you that your sister intercepted and blew up your house. The Colonel ordered it all."

Ray shouted, "Rose, go back in the house. She's delusional."

Rose aimed the gun at Ray. "I'll shoot, Colonel. You shot my Andre in the back. Throw your gun to the ground, or I'll blow your fucking head off."

Mason shouted, "Go back in the house. Please, Rose."

In the distance, more sirens and police lights drew near the tractor lane.

Logan shouted, "Ray? You're the Colonel?"

Alex made the connection. That was why there had been no arrests. The pieces of the puzzle fell into place. Adrenaline coursed through his body. He had to get to Lauren.

In a split second, Ray pulled back the hammer of his gun.

Rose rushed forward and slipped on the icy steps, releasing the gun into the air with a spray of bullets.

Pandemonium broke out with screams, shouts, and gunshots, and everything seemed to go in slow motion.

Bratten appeared next to Alex. "Get Mason."

Alex didn't have time to analyze the best course of action. He couldn't stop the whizzing of bullets. His only thoughts were to cover Lauren and save her life. Alex and Bratten lunged forward, yanking Lauren out of Mason's hands and throwing her to the ground.

Mason fired at Alex, hitting him once in the shoulder, knocking Alex off balance.

The following bullet hit Alex's thigh. The drumming of his heart seemed to catch in his throat.

At first, Alex didn't feel anything until the bullet exited with unbearable pain. The fire shredded his muscles and a roar released from his mouth. Hot blood gushed from the wound, making the snow turn red.

The snow tapered off into light flurries. The air stilled as Alex dropped to the ground. He disconnected from everything except Lauren's face.

She crawled to him on her hands and knees. He couldn't understand her muffled words.

He felt like he was swimming underwater.

The pain ebbed and faded as Alex looked at Bratten's face. Then his gaze went to Lauren when his spirit separated from his body, hovering next to Bratten. "Am I dead?"

Bratten said, "I'm here, my old friend. We are one." His arms circled Alex, and he pointed to Lauren. "Her tears are for you now." Bratten slammed his palms against Alex's chest.

With a sudden and profound intake of breath, Alex's spirit reconnected to his body with searing pain. A rush of people surrounded him. He drifted out of consciousness.

Tears rolled down Lauren's face. Her eyes went wide, watching the paramedics work on him, her fist in her mouth as if stifling a scream.

She was safe.

Nothing else mattered.

Chapter 16

From the time Lauren climbed out of the cellar and Mason grabbed her by the neck, pressing a gun to her head, she'd watched helplessly as the events unfolded in mere minutes.

Detective Stone had killed Bratten. His alias known as The Colonel.

Then everything happened super fast. Rose slipped on the ice, and her gun went off, then Logan shot Detective Stone.

Bratten materialized next to Alex as they rushed Mason. Alex took two hits, falling to the ground. She turned and screamed for help and watched Logan shoot Mason three times in the chest. Then he went to Rose.

Trembling, Lauren crawled to her knees and pressed her hands over the gunshot wound on Alex's thigh, but blood spread in a pool turning the white snow red. She couldn't breathe. Her stomach churned and clenched with fear. Fear of losing Alex.

She looked at him and cried, "I love you, Alex. Please don't leave me."

Alex's eyes seemed unfocused, looking at her with a blank stare, and she screamed again, "Someone help me, please. He's dying."

Logan raced to Alex, pushing Lauren out of the way and placing his belt around Alex's upper thigh to stop the bleeding. He spoke calmly to Alex. "It's going to be okay, buddy. Hang in there. Come on, Alex, fight. Stay with me."

The glimmer of red and blue lights swirling along with the wailing and changing pitch of the sirens brought her hope of saving Alex's life, but Lauren looked at Bratten. He shook his head back and forth. Alex turned deathly pale.

She screamed, "No. Please, God, don't take Alex too. Please save him. Do something, Bratten. Save him."

The paramedics rushed in and reacted quickly, removing Alex's pant leg to locate the wound.

Logan wrapped her in his coat and pulled her away. She clawed at him. "No. I'm staying with Alex. Let me go, Logan."

Logan stayed almost insanely calm. "You aren't helping him if you don't allow the paramedics to do their job."

The TBI and federal agents arrived, and Logan methodically relayed the events. "I need a car."

Special Agent Woods looked at one of the TBI agents and said, "Take Logan and Ms. Drake wherever they need to go. I'll stay to secure the location while CSI gathers evidence." He turned to Logan and said, "We executed the warrants with the sheriff's department. It's a joint investigation with the TBI, and a total of five searches are underway, including The Dirty Rat. We have them, Logan."

Lauren's voice quivered. "One of them is bound in the cellar. His name is T-bone."

Special Agent Woods nodded.

"Take me to the hospital, please. I need to be with Alex." A calm settled over her as she watched the ambulance leave with Alex."

"I'm Special Agent Osborne. I'll take you to the hospital. Mrs. Drake, you need to go to the ER too."

"I'm fine. I want to be with Alex."

Special Agent Osborne said, "Logan, do you mind?" He pointed to the back of the police car. Logan entered the back-seat while Osborne opened the passenger door for Lauren. She slid into the car. Someone handed him a blanket, and he placed it over Lauren.

On the way back to Eagle Creek, Logan and Jeff talked, but she didn't listen. She couldn't think of anything except Alex.

She prayed silently.

Dear Lord, forgive me for my shortcomings. I'm unworthy of your blessings, but I beg of you, please have your warrior angels surround Alex. Place your healing hand on Alex. Make him well. Please, oh, Lord, I love him. Please, please don't take him too.

She repeated the prayer like a mantra.

Arriving at the hospital, Lauren glanced at her blood-soaked clothing and grimaced. Alex's blood. Logan ushered her into the emergency room. The ambulance had already arrived, and Alex was in the O.R.

Déjà vu.

Lauren would never get over Bratten's death. She pushed the similarities away. She couldn't go there. Alex would survive. She hugged herself and rocked back and forth in the waiting room chair. Logan tried to comfort her, but Lauren didn't want to talk. She kept her prayer vigil.

Angeline rushed into the waiting room with Eron and swept Lauren in her arms, crying. "Thank God you're alive."

Lauren frowned and pushed her away. "Don't worry about me. Pray for Alex. I can't lose him, Angeline. I can't."

Hours passed when the surgeon stepped out of the double doors. He said, "Is there someone from the Alex Charland family here?"

Lauren squeezed Logan's hand and walked to the surgeon.

He said, "Mr. Charland is alive." The rest of the surgeon's description of Alex's condition went over her head.

Her heart swelled with love. She cried tears of joy, tears of thanksgiving.

Alex was alive.

Days went by slowly. Lauren only left Alex's side long enough to change clothes. She slept on the couch in his room that let out into a bed and dozed restlessly. She hadn't seen his green eyes since he'd rescued her.

Walking over to the wall window, Lauren looked out over the hills of Eagle Creek, watching the deep orange hues of sunrise as the evening stars gave way to daylight.

Alex moaned, and she rushed to his side.

"Honey, are you awake?" She held his hand.

"Lauren?"

She pressed the nurse's button. "Alex is awake. Hurry. He's awake."

"What happened?" he said groggily.

Lauren was afraid to tell Alex too much. The doctor had suggested that she allow him to remember the events independently. "You're okay. That's the only thing that matters."

Alex struggled to swallow as the nurse came into the room. "Good morning, Mr. Charland. How are you feeling this morning?"

"Hurt," he gasped.

"Yes. I'm sure you hurt. I can give you something for pain."

He shook his head. "No. I don't want to sleep anymore. Lauren?"

"I'm here, honey. I'm right here."

The nurse checked his vitals, and a tech came in and took his blood. After the doctor on call checked his wound, he said, "Things look good. No infection. No fever. Mr. Charland, I think you're going to be okay."

After the doctor left, Alex said, "Mason? Detective Stone?"

"They died at the farm." She told him of the events. "Rose is turning state's evidence. The FBI raided The Revolutionist Brotherhood cell, and the remaining brothers are in jail."

Alex closed his eyes for a long minute.

With a slight smile, he said, "Good." He rubbed his hand over the top of hers. His breathing was ragged. "I saw Bratten. He was there when I died. I think he saved me."

Lauren said, "I saw him too."

Alex seemed relieved. "Is he still here?"

She smiled and reached over to his hand. "I think he's moved on."

His eyes searched hers. "What is it?"

"Will you marry me?"

He chuckled. "You want to marry me?"

"Don't laugh. I don't want to waste time not telling you how I feel. I love you, Alex. I want to marry you." Her grin went wide.

He frowned. "What's my prognosis?"

"And that matters, how?"

Shaking his head, he stuttered, "Not, not going to burden you."

"You heard the doctor. You're going to be okay. You had some nerve and tissue damage in your thigh, but no bones were fractured. You wore an FBI coat that day. The bullet that hit your shoulder melted into the coat. It didn't penetrate. The surgeon said you might experience some pain in your thigh during the healing process, but you're healing nicely. The rehab therapist has stopped by a few times to check on you."

"How long have I been out?"

"Four days, twelve hours, and forty-five minutes."

He said, "Yes."

Her brows popped. "Yes?"

"I want to marry you. I want your babies too."

Lauren lowered the hospital rail and removed the oxygen from his nose, then leaned in and kissed him softly on his lips.

Alex moaned. "I want to go home."

Lauren brushed Alex's hair away from his forehead and pressed a kiss. "That's an excellent sign."

Lauren married Alex in a civil ceremony conducted by a judge friend of Alex's who held their ceremony in his chambers. It was short, sweet, and beautiful.

She wore a simple white dress with tiny flowers braided in her hair. Alex wore a spring suit that brought out the gold in his green eyes. Angeline and Eron were witnesses.

Since Alex was still recuperating, Lauren demanded honeymooning in his bedroom's comfort. They vegged out on old movies, and she started cooking healthier meals. Every day, she helped him, and every day he became stronger.

She gave over the reins of Drake Properties to Eron until Alex recovered.

Weeks turned into months, Lauren and Alex bought one of the first finished homes in Wycliffe Commons.

They met Eron to go over the final inspection before moving in.

Her hands slid over the brown, gray, and cream sparkling quartz countertops. "Gorgeous, Eron. I love the counters."

"Yeah, they're less costly and more durable than their granite counterparts." Eron's back pressed against the center island. "Pendants look great too."

She looked overhead at the stylish pendant lights that hung over the bar. "Eron, you saved us a small fortune." Alex leaned against the cabinets holding onto his cane.

"Aw, shucks, sis. I'd do it for free if I could." He reached into his pocket. "Here's your key. I have an extra. I figure you and Angeline might want to set up the kitchen first. I'm wrapping up for the day. Angeline has dinner ready, so I'm heading home."

She giggled, thinking of her sister's demands on dinnertime simultaneously every night. "Oh, I love the gray cabinets and the warm wood accents." She reached up and kissed Alex on the mouth and winked. His grin went wide.

Eron said, "The pullout drawers and racks saved you big bucks, and there's no wasted shelving. Have to run. You guys be safe."

"Tell Angeline I'll call her."

Eron gingerly kissed her forehead. "Love you, both."

"Love you too." She watched Eron leave the house. She tipped Alex's chin with her forefinger. "If you're hurting, we can go."

The natural light from the windows made his eyes flicker. "Um. Let's see the rest of the house first. Kiss me again. That always makes me feel better."

She reached up, circled his neck, and kissed him. "I'll call the movers and set up a time to move us. I'll try to get the move done over a long weekend."

His fingers entwined with hers. "Works. I feel so freaking helpless."

Lauren frowned. "You are not helpless. I intend to put you to work on the sofa wrapping glassware and plates." She looked around at the house and then looked up into Alex's eyes.

"Eron did a fantastic job." He pulled her into his arms, and she wrapped her arms around his waist.

"Yes, he did," replied Lauren.

The most extravagant expense was the main bedroom and bathroom upstairs, leading to a covered balcony overlooking the golf course.

It took Alex a little extra time to navigate the stairwell.

She said, "We can set up the bedroom downstairs until you're better."

"No. I'm getting better. The harder I work, the quicker I'll heal."

She opened the French doors and looked at the backyard. "Good. I still want to beat you at golf."

Alex stepped up behind Lauren. "I'm sure you do, and I still want you to run a marathon with me."

"Ugh. Not sure I'm ready for a marathon." Lauren ran her hands through his hair and trailed them down his muscled biceps. "I think..."

"What were you thinking?" he asked with a raised brow.

"I think we should christen each room of the house, starting in our bedroom, but I don't want to hurt you." Lauren grabbed Alex's hand, coaxing him into the large bathroom.

Alex moaned with delight. "Sounds great to me. Hurt me, please."

Fluttering filled her belly as she gazed into his eyes. Every time Alex looked at her, Lauren knew she'd been given a great gift. Lauren reached for his hand and pressed the back to her cheek. "I love you."

She watched emotions cross his face. His eyes smoldered as he pushed her against the bathroom wall. With a hoarse whisper, he said, "Lauren, I love you too, but we may have to improvise." He looked at the Jacuzzi tub and the bay window with a cushioned seat. "Ah. Perfect." He laid his cane down and gave her *the look*.

That's all it took.

Lauren's breathing became heavy. Her knees trembled, nearly buckling beneath her as she pressed her body next to his as he lowered to the seat pressing his back against the wall.

He took her hands and turned them, kissing her palms. Sad eyes looked at her through thick black lashes. "It cost us a lot to be here, but something great bloomed out of something so tragic."

She slid in beside him on his good side. "We made it, though."

Alex cradled her head in his hand. "I love you, wife."

The air crackled and thickened between them, uncurling a ribbon of desire. A thousand thoughts pinged Lauren's brain while Alex kissed her.

He didn't say another word, just dragged her onto his lap, pulling her close, his warm breath on her neck, as he slowly unbuttoned her shirt.

Chapter 17

Lauren and Alex moved into their new home at Wycliffe Commons. Spring had turned into summer. The warm breeze blew her hair off her shoulders as she squinted into the bright sunshine.

She walked with Alex along the golf cart path at dusk next to a babbling stream. He still needed a cane, but his leg grew stronger every day. She held Alex's hand tight as rolling laughter escaped his mouth, and golden specks in his green eyes flickered.

Alex retold a favorite story about him and Bratten during their college days, and Lauren closed her eyes, visualizing Bratten.

She didn't feel his presence anymore.

Bratten disappeared the day Alex was shot.

She prayed Bratten was at peace. She would love him forever.

The love for Alex was on an entirely different level. Her passion for Alex was a slow-burning kind of love grown out of respect and friendship, and through time, her love for Alex matured and deepened into something incredibly hot and sensual.

Love with Alex, beautiful and sweet.

Alex Charland. The tall, dark, and incredibly handsome attorney. He was a man of few words, but the words he spoke left an impression—a gentleman who melted her heart with love, kindness, and compassion.

Lauren never dreamed of loving another person. Love's a funny thing. She never planned on falling in love. It just happened. Love could be painful, and the sky soaring at other times. Love was blindingly beautiful if one surrendered to it. An interesting concept, surrendering to love meant losing control over her emotions.

Allowing herself to love again was frightening.

She had vowed never to love again after Bratten died.

Love had other ideas.

During the weeks and months following the shooting. Alex set up therapy sessions with a psychiatrist to deal with the trauma for him and Lauren.

One summer afternoon, after moving into their new home, Alex grabbed a booth next to the window at See You Latte located on the square of the quaint and charming Wycliffe.

He'd ordered a chai tea and waited for Lauren to arrive. He hoped her session with Dr. Webster went well. The doc had helped him through many transitions he'd experienced over the last year.

Dr. Webster had talked him down from the ledge, metaphorically speaking a couple of times with his chronic pain from the gunshot wound. He and Lauren had suffered much, but both agreed the therapy sessions helped.

Lauren pulled into a parking spot next to his car, spotted him as she got out of the car, and waved.

He grinned and threw up his hand in greeting.

Watching her walk into the coffee shop filled his heart with so much love, and she seemed ecstatically happy. The session must've gone great.

Lauren slid across from him and grabbed a menu. "I'm starving." She briefly looked at him and smiled. "Do we order at the counter or what?"

Alex pushed the chair back and stood. "I'll go order. What do you want?"

"Hmm. I think chicken noodle soup, grill cheese, and a coke. Oh, make that a glass of milk and hot apple pie with vanilla ice cream for dessert." She closed the menu and placed it back behind the napkin dispenser.

He shook his head. "Somebody's hungry."

As he walked off, he heard Lauren say playfully, "What do you expect when someone's pregnant?"

He froze, spun around, and sprinted back to the table. "What? Are you? Are we?"

She nodded. "Yup. I didn't meet with Dr. Webster today. I met with Dr. Gross, my new OBGYN. We're pregnant." She practically jumped into his arms, and he swung her around, kissing her all over her face.

"You okay?"

"I'm fine. I'm still hungry, though." She laughed.

He walked to the counter on a cloud. A baby. He couldn't wait to be a father. He ordered, and the cashier gave him a number and told him they'd bring the order to the table.

Alex slid into the booth and frowned. "Are you sure that you're okay? You have a funny look on your face."

Lauren's grin grew wide. "You're not using your cane."

Epilogue

Fifteen months later

Wycliffe Avenue Ribbon Cutting Ceremony

Lauren sat on the decorated platform with Alex, Riley Gates, Brady Weber, and Rick Kirkland as Mayor Lane addressed the crowd at the Wycliffe Avenue Grand Opening Ceremony.

"Wycliffe Avenue embodies the character of our city. The project scope has developed an array of high-end shops and galleries, and we've managed to land a luxury hotel due to open by fall. The eighteen-hole golf course launched earlier in the year with the new community of homes and condos. The greenways connect to the downtown trailheads to our historic square."

Mayor Lane's voice boomed over the loudspeaker system. "I'd be remiss if I didn't mention that Wycliffe Avenue was the brainchild of the late Mr. Bratten Drake. He was a true visionary, and through Lauren and Alex Charland, his dreams were more than realized. They are a great success. That's why I'm proud to unveil the lifelike bronze sculpture of Mr. Drake to live on in his hometown of Wycliffe."

Lauren choked up with tears as they unveiled Bratten's statue, and Alex reached over and squeezed her hand. She looked out at the crowd. On the front row sat her family. She smiled, and her heart nearly burst with pride.

Mayor Lane continued, "Please enjoy the day's festivities and a quick reminder of the town dance this evening on the green in the town square. Seize the day, my friends."

Lauren and Alex shook hands and spoke with town dignitaries as they made their way to the front row, where Angeline held their pride and joy.

"Thanks, sis."

"Thank *you*. I love this child."

Lauren reached out with her hands and said, "Bratten, it's mama."

The baby boy's ocean blue eyes widened, and he clapped his hands together. "Ma-ma."

She pulled him into her arms, kissing him as he wrapped his chubby arms around her neck. His dark chestnut hair ruffled against her nose.

Alex leaned in and said, "What about me? Don't I get any?"

Bratten jumped up and down in her arms. "Da-dee. Da-dee." He reached for Alex, who took him and raised him high in the sky to the squeals and peals of baby laughter.

Lauren giggled.

Alex laughed too. "Come on, baby. I have all kinds of fun lined up for us today."

The sun shone brightly over their heads. Lauren breathed a deep sigh as she followed father and son. She thanked God and looked at the blue sky, blowing a kiss. "Thank you for my happily ever after, again."

Bratten, Nancy, and Aunt Lynda watched the happy family melt into the crowds of people among the Wycliffe Avenue's shops. He'd watched the love grow between his two favorite people on earth.

He looked at Nancy, then Aunt Lynda. "So, the boy looks a little like me, huh?"

Nancy giggled. "He does have your blue eyes."

"How did that happen?"

Aunt Lynda leaned against Bratten's shoulder. "Transference. You saved Alex."

"So, the baby is mine too?" He grinned.

"In a way, we all belong to each other, son," Nancy replied.

Bratten stepped in between Nancy and Aunt Lynda, offering his arm to each. "Are we going to see the great and powerful Oz?"

He threw his head back and laughed as the veil of light opened, and they walked through to the next dimension. He chuckled. "Are we following the yellow brick road to his emerald castle?"

Nancy patted his hand. "I love your sense of humor, son. It's much better than Oz."

He dipped his chin. "Really? So, am I the Scarecrow, the Tin Man, or the Lion?"

Aunt Lynda laughed. "You have brains."

Nancy leaned in and added, "Lots of courage and, most importantly, a generous heart."

He grinned as they faded into the heavens. "Then take me home, Dorothy."

Excerpt

The WItches of Hant Hollow 3: Frostville

Prologue

Iris shook her head in hopes of ridding herself of the memories from the night everything went wrong. Her need for revenge had clouded her judgment so intensely that nothing else mattered.

She had gone so far as to have betrayed her family, the Doanharts. The disbelief and terror expressed in her family's eyes would haunt her for the rest of her life. Her family had risked their lives to warn her of future events and even changed the historical timeline to give her a second chance.

What did she do to repay their sacrifice?

She killed a mortal man.

Why? It boiled down to one word. *Jealousy.*

On that fateful night in Paris, Iris tried to tell them she was sorry and share her secret, how Valdoor, her biological grandfather, had cast her under his spell. She was bound to him through dark magic. He knew her thoughts sometimes before she did. In an instant, with a flick of his wrist, he transported Iris from Hagatha's home, and she materialized into a locked room in a realm he created called Frostville.

Iris couldn't blame her entire plight on Valdoor. She had used blood magic against her foes for nearly a century.

Light and dark forces were available to any witch, wizard, or magical being. Still, taking a mortal's life intentionally without it being in self-defense required Iris to sever ties with her coven and the Mage Alliance, Earth's governing body over supernatural beings.

Valdoor had offered her a place at his side to rule the dark world with some of the most dangerous beings with one purpose. He intended to conquer the Mage Alliance and return to the Pleiades star cluster, their birthplace, as soon as his army had sufficient numbers.

Of late, Iris began having second thoughts about Valdoor's vision. He had used her maliciously since she'd become spellbound, and most of the time, she couldn't remember the depth of the depravity she had inflicted on others.

She possessed powerful magic, but would that be enough to stop him?

Doubtful, unless she could persuade the Doanhart Coven to help her, and if they agreed, maybe the Mage Alliance too. If only she could escape the room, go to Valdoor's library, steal his grimoire, and take it to her family. Beg them for forgiveness, then maybe they had a chance of binding him forever.

The portal door suddenly energized.

She held her hands, palms up, then chanted, "Duplicate the entry sequence, and store the memory in my safe place." She memorized each long thin beam of light using a translocation spell as it entered the magicked room.

Valdoor's army commander, Orphic, materialized in front of her.

She painted on a fake smile and tucked her hands into her coat pockets before he could see she manipulated magic.

Iris sensed the hostility inside the warlock. And she knew Orphic wanted to marry her. She planned on escaping before he asked for her hand.

She doubted Valdoor would agree to their match anyway. She was, after all, a purebred goddess of Pleiades and Orion.

"I brought tea and the cakes you like." His leer gave her the creeps. He placed the silver service tray on the white oak side table next to two maroon wingback chairs.

She tamped down her repulsion and replied in a sweet voice, "Thank you."

"Have you been able to sleep?"

"Intermittently. The tea helps. Would you care to join me?"

His grin widened. "Yes, thank you."

"I'll pour," she said. "Do you like sugar and cream?"

He took a seat in the chair. "A little of both, please."

Iris needed information, so she conjured a truth serum and sprinkled it into his tea.

She handed him the cup and then sat opposite him. "Has Valdoor returned?"

"You don't need to worry your pretty little head over him." Orphic slurped. "I promise I won't allow anything to happen to you."

"How's your tea?"

"Perfect." He gulped it.

She gritted her teeth. Tea was supposed to be savored and not devoured like a tankard of ale.

"How long does Valdoor intend to hold me prisoner?" She tapped her foot in agitation.

"You're not a prisoner." He leaned over and squeezed her knee. "We believe the Mage Alliance has placed spies within our ranks. You're in here for protection only."

"I would like to speak with Valdoor."

"Not possible. He's away until tomorrow."

The time had come to put her plan into action. "I am more than capable of holding my own, Orphic" She placed her hand over his. "I don't need a babysitter."

I love your fiery spirit." He kissed the back of her hand. "With your permission, I'd like to ask Valdoor for your hand in marriage."

Over my dead body. "Then prove it." She placed her cup on the table and wet her lips. "Show me how to get out of this room, take me to Valdoor's library, and I'll give you anything you want."

He pulled her to a standing position and drew her against him. "Anything?"

She lowered her lids. "Anything, Orphic."

"Look to the four corners of the room. You'll see an overlapping in the design. It's like a screen protector. Just lift the edge of the veil to escape." With a husky whisper, he said, "But a warning, sensors are in place to alert security. Valdoor has issued an order to kill you on the spot should you escape. Follow me."

She took his face in her hands and kissed him—not any kiss, a kiss of subjugation, one that gave her power over Orphic's will. "I'll follow you."

Chapter 1

Judson McKay gazed out his corner window office. His father, the reigning king of The McKay Corporation, had died suddenly from an aneurysm, throwing their family and the business into chaos. As Judson tried to reconcile the loss of his father, he turned to the lead attorney with the firm, Dewey Carlisle.

"Judson, your father, um," Dewey coughed. "Atticus named Everett as president of the McKay Corporation."

Judson struggled to breathe.

He'd worked eighty hours a week for the business for the last fifteen years. Surely that had meant something to his dynasty-obsessed father. He and his father butted heads often, but Dad had hinted more than once that he'd run the company someday.

Evidently not.

Had Judson made some monumental mistake and didn't know it?

The immediate family's wealth exceeded more than they would ever need in two lifetimes. Atticus had built his fortune in steel before relocating to Nashville in the late eighties. He then diversified the company's holdings into mining, banking, media, telecom, and recent acquisitions in technology. Still, getting to the heart of the matter, Judson's success in business and life tied intricately with his father and the corporation.

Had Atticus ever loved him or respected him? *I guess not as much as Everett.*

I'm not working for my kid brother.

"Thanks for letting me know, Dewey." Judson left the conference room for the last time, shoulders back, chin lifted, he strode out of McKay Tower. He'd resign to Everett at home. They were close, and both had poured blood, sweat, and tears into building the family fortune under Atticus's iron fists.

There had to be something more to life than work, and he intended on finding it.

On one hundred and forty acres, Judson drove into the McKay's affluent estate outside Franklin, Tennessee. He parked his black 911 Porsche in the circular drive and lumbered up to his suite.

He took off his suit and hung it in the walk-in closet. He took a scorching hot shower. After dressing into jeans and a navy-blue crewneck sweater, he stared into the flickering flames of the double-sided fireplace that separated the sitting area from the king-size four-poster bed.

His mother, Delilah, knocked lightly on his door and stuck her head inside. "May I come in?" She walked in without him replying.

"Darling, how are you?" In her mid-fifties, his mother was still beautiful. Dark hair pulled tight in a loose bun, red lipstick, and fingernails, complexion clear and unblemished.

Judson raised a brow. "How do you think? Wanna drink?"

"No, honey. It's a little early for cocktails." Delilah sat in one of the white tufted reading chairs next to the fire. "I need to explain what happened with Dewey this morning. It's my fault. All of it."

"How is it your fault?" He stepped over to the built-in bar area and grabbed one of the crystal snifters. "It's not about the money, Mom. It's about Atticus digging into my craw from beyond the grave. He lied to me."

Delilah's face softened. "Well, Atticus didn't lie to you. I did." She crossed her ankles and slid them slightly to the right. Her posture and pose were picture-perfect.

"What did you lie about?" Judson plopped into the white chair opposite her.

Delilah glanced down and twisted her diamond wedding ring around her finger. "I don't want to lose you, but you deserve the truth. I loved your father, but I was a different person before we married. I ..."

Judson sipped brandy. His fingertip ran along the rim of the glass. "Okay, you're making me nervous. Just tell me."

"You won't believe me."

"I will believe you. Just spit it out, Mom."

She reached over and patted his knee. "I'm a witch."

"Good one." Judson laughed out loud.

"I'm not lying. I can prove it." She wiggled her forefinger, and his cocktail glass vanished.

He frowned, tilting his head to the side.

WTH!

"See, your father knew so little about me. I tried to tell him, but he swept me off my feet. He was so charming. We flew to Vegas and got married in one of those Elvis chapels. I didn't know it at the time, but I was already pregnant with you." She stood.

A sick feeling churned in the pit of Justin's gut.

She gave a long sigh. "Your birth father, Preston Novak, presented himself at our front door the day before your father died. He had dreamed you were in danger, some sort of life-changing trouble brewing. Witches and wizards never ignore omens. He felt a strong connection to you and demanded that I tell him if you were his son. He said it was the only way to protect you from the dark forces." She paused and took another breath. "I couldn't lie anymore. Preston knew the truth anyway. He just wanted to hear it from me." Her shoulders slumped.

"Well, don't that beat the band. No wonder Atticus gave Everett control of the company. I'm a bastard." His intense anger threatened his composure. "Am I a wizard or witch? I can't do magic, so I must be a mongrel. Thanks for nothing."

She paced back and forth in front of the fireplace, wringing her hands. "I was barely twenty and engaged to Preston when I met Atticus. I had no clue I was pregnant."

"Great, you were sleeping with two men at the same time. I guess the apple doesn't fall far from the tree, eh?"

Delilah frowned. "Don't be impertinent, Judson. I cannot abide you speaking to me using that tone regardless of the situation. I never cheated on Atticus, not once. I broke off the engagement to Preston after I met him. Preston followed us to Vegas and approached me in the hotel room. I explained I never meant to hurt him. While I loved Preston, I was not in love with him. Atticus stole my heart."

She stopped pacing and gazed into the flickering flames. "See, Preston and I grew up together. We were more friends than lovers. But the minute I saw Atticus, I knew I could never marry Preston. I begged him to accept my decision. His eyes filled with tears. He told me he'd love me for the rest of his life. For a warlock, that's an extremely long time. I never spoke to Preston again until last week."

She looked at Judson. "I placed a protection spell on you as a baby. Better for you to grow up as a mortal." She swallowed hard. Tears filled her eyes. "When I presented Preston to Atticus and finally told him the truth, he became enraged. He screamed and fell to the floor, clutching his chest. By the time the ambulance arrived, Atticus had passed away."

"What do you want me to say? That I forgive you? How can you forgive yourself?" He shouted, "Because I don't know if I can. I need time and distance."

"I hold myself responsible. I've ruined everything." She stepped over to the window and dabbed her eyes. "I'm sorry, Judson. I did the best I could. I never wanted to hurt you. I didn't want to hurt anyone."

"Where does my real father live?"

"Wooddale Farms."

"Never heard of it. Where is it?" Judson pressed his lips into a tight line.

"Not too far from here. He lives in Rutherford County, next to Hant Hollow. The communities of Wooddale and Hant Hollow are safe havens for supernatural beings, away from mortal interference. And there's a door to another realm called Waytherlands." Her face softened. "I haven't thought of Waytherlands in decades. It's a beautiful ethereal place."

Judson withdrew his phone and entered the town's name in his search engine. "I can't find it. I want to meet him. I deserve to know my biological father. Please, give me Preston's address."

Delilah cupped his face with her hands. "Open your eyes, my child, and allow the forces of light to reconcile your heart and soul. Open your mind to magic. May the Goddess of Light protect you, Judson." She stepped back.

The room seemed to breathe around him. Sparks of light flickered in his vision like rays shooting from the sun. Judson couldn't understand fully what had just happened, but he changed.

Everett walked into the room and joined them near the hearth. "I could cut the tension in this room with a knife. Is it about the meeting today? Judson, man, please don't be mad at me. We can work together. We'll figure out the logistics as we go along."

A wave of fiery power flowed through him, like nothing he had ever experienced before. Suddenly, he knew the path he'd been on all his life was no longer the one he wanted. On the verge of emotional upheaval, Judson hugged his brother. "I love you, Everett, but I don't want to work at McKay. I don't want to live in this house anymore." He turned to Delilah. "I'm going to find my real father."

Everett's eyes widened. "What?"

"Mom will give you the details. If you two will excuse me, I have packing to do."

Everett looked at Delilah. "What's Judson talking about?"

Judson felt his mother's hand on his forearm.

He jerked away from her. She had hidden the truth from him for too long.

"I hope one day you will forgive me, son. I love you so much."

Thank you for reading my excerpt. Please consider purchasing. For buy links: go to DFJonesAuthor.com

About the Author

USA Today bestselling author D.F. Jones landed her dream job shortly after college as a broadcast consultant at the ABC Affiliate in Nashville, which led her to open an advertising agency. Over the decades, she's created many campaigns for clients, but in 2015, she fell in love with writing.

Her books offer fun and fast-paced action with romantic elements, whether it's angels and demons, time travel, witches, or ghost
mysteries.

She's happily married to the love of her life and best friend, KJ. She loves to laugh, and he keeps her in stitches. They have two
gorgeous grown sons that she loves and adores more than life itself.

D.F. Jones is a fan of the Tennessee Titans, MTSU Blue Raiders, and she enjoys working in her flower gardens.

Register for her newsletter and read a book for free go to: https://dfjonesauthor.com/register-for-updates

Follow on social media: https://dfjonesauthor.com/social media

Also By

D.F. Jones, USA Today bestselling author
For Buy Links and info on preorders:
DFJonesAuthor.com

Ditch Lane Diaries 4 Book Collection

Ruby's Choice: The Dreamer (Book 1) FREE at most digital stores

Anna's Way: The Healer (Book 2)

Sandy's Story: The Soul Reader (Book 3)

Lee's Lesson: Warrior Angel (Book 4)

Angel Watcher (A Ditch Lane Diaries Short)

Angel Watcher (audiobook)

The Witches of Hant Hollow 1: Jonathan's Curse

The Witches of Hant Hollow 2: Gate Keepers

The Witches of Hant Hollow 3: Frostville

Spinning Time (A Time Travel Romance)

ATTRA Chronicles1 (a Spinning Time Novella)

Happily Ever After, Again: A Ghost Mystery

'Tis The Season: Sweet Romance Novelettes FREE at most
digital Stores
Thank you for supporting my work!